HOW COULD THIS BE HAPPENING?

With a sigh, Laurie opened her math book and looked at the first problems. As she stared at the numbers in their neat rows, suddenly they seemed to go in and out of focus. Frowning, she squinted hard. But her head felt strange—there was a muffled roaring sound in her ears. For a moment she felt as if a giant fishbowl had been inverted over her head, skewing her vision. And then she heard again the voice that had cried out during the night. "Please, help me!"

Laurie's head jerked up and she looked around in a panic. No one else seemed to have heard anything—the heads of her classmates were bent over their books. Involuntarily she turned toward the windows at the back of the classroom. Could a child be outside? But no, if a child were crying out there, Laurie would still be hearing him.

With heavy certainty Laurie knew that it was the same voice that had awakened her the night before. And she was still convinced it wasn't something she'd imagined—it was too real for that. Yet how could it be real?

Berkley Books by Beverly Hastings

DON'T TALK TO STRANGERS
DON'T WALK HOME ALONE
SOMEBODY HELP ME
WATCHER IN THE DARK

SOMEBODY HELP ME

BEVERLY HASTINGS

BERKLEY BOOKS, NEW YORK

SOMEBODY HELP ME

A Berkley Book / published by arrangement with the authors

PRINTING HISTORY
Berkley edition / September 1993

For information address: The Berkley Publishing Group, 200 Madison Avenue, New York, New York 10016.

ISBN: 0-425-13906-9

A BERKLEY BOOK ® TM 757,375
Berkley Books are published by
The Berkley Publishing Group,
200 Madison Avenue, New York, New York 10016.
The name "BERKLEY" and the "B" logo
are trademarks belonging to
Berkley Publishing Corporation.

PRINTED IN THE UNITED STATES OF AMERICA

10 9 8 7 6 5 4 3 2 1

For Natalee, with thanks for your understanding

CHAPTER 1

"HELP ME! OH, PLEASE, HELP ME!"

Laurie lay rigid under the covers, her eyes wide open and staring into the blackness. Fear washed over her, turning her hands and feet icy cold. She tried to rub her hands together to warm them up, but she couldn't seem to move.

Gradually the outlines of her bedroom window appeared as the moonlight filtered in pale gleams through the curtains. Now she knew where she was—at home in her own room. But the only noises she could hear were the familiar swishing of wind in the trees outside and the rumbling purr of her cat, Casey, who lay curled neatly in the exact middle of the bed. What had awakened her?

"Oh, please, help me!" The words echoed in her mind. It was the voice of a young child, and the sound was so thin and pitiful, Laurie could hardly bear it. Unwanted, a picture sprang into her mind of a little boy, lost, terrified, and hopeless. She could hear him calling again: "Help me!"

Laurie's muscles ached from lying so stiff and still. It took all her willpower to sit up and focus on the glowing numbers of her bedside clock. Three-ten in the morning—she'd been sleeping soundly for hours before that pathetic cry had jarred her awake.

Protesting at the unexpected disturbance of his comfortable nest, Casey glared at Laurie, then yawned and stretched. He stepped carefully into her lap and began kneading his paws to make a suitably rumpled new space. Automatically Laurie rubbed the soft fur behind his ears, grateful for the warm reality of his compact body. But even the touch of his rough tongue on her arm couldn't distract her from the sad little voice she'd heard. Who could be calling for help?

The house Laurie lived in with her dad had been built only five years ago. Set apart from its neighbors on a wooded hillside, it had a separate, almost isolated feeling. And no one who lived nearby had young children. Perhaps one of the neighbors had visitors, Laurie thought, and a child who didn't know the area very well had gotten lost in the dark. But even as she clutched at this explanation Laurie knew it didn't make sense. If some little kid was lost outside at three in the morning, people would be out looking for him. There would be sounds of people talking to one another and calling the child's name.

The silence outside her window told Laurie

that there was no lost child anywhere nearby. So it must have been a dream, she thought. Just lie down and forget it and go back to sleep.

Obeying her own instructions, Laurie lay down and pulled the covers back up around her shoulders. The night was chilly for early October, a foretaste of the cold weather to come. But though she closed her eyes, her brain refused to stop churning.

It was just a dream, dummy, she insisted to herself. But deep down she knew that it wasn't. The voice was too real. And she could still hear it clearly in her mind—not like those images and sounds in dreams that begin to fade as soon as the dreamer awakes. What she had heard was a desperately sad child crying for help. But who, and where? And how could she have heard something that wasn't anywhere in hearing distance? Laurie didn't have the answers to these questions, but she still felt certain that the terrified voice of a little child had awakened her just a few minutes ago.

You're letting your imagination run away with you, Laurie, she told herself firmly. This echo of her father's frequent exasperated comment should have been comforting—after all, if it was only in her imagination, it wasn't important. But lying there with her eyes scrunched shut, Laurie couldn't make herself believe that the voice was just a product of her own fantasies. She knew that somehow, somewhere, it was real. With dull certainty she thought, And I know I'll hear it again.

Scared and bewildered, Laurie lay in bed and waited for dawn.

CHAPTER 2

A SINISTER VOICE WHISPERED IN Laurie's ear. "Waiting for someone, sweetheart?"

Spinning around, she was trapped by two strong arms. For a moment she struggled, her heart beating wildly. Then she realized. "Oh, Chuck, you scared me!"

He gave her shoulders a little shake and looked down into her face with his charming grin. "Little scaredy-cat Laurie," he said in a mocking tone. "Too scared of big bad Chuck to go get some lunch?"

Laurie smiled at him and pushed her straight dark hair away from her face. "Of course not—I'm starving! And I think my brain cells need food. Mr. Bilakian seems to think we can learn the whole chemistry course in the first two months."

"It's your own fault for taking it," Chuck said as he steered Laurie through the heavy exit doors of Granville High School. "You should drop chem and take sculpture like me. Miss

Vandrum is happy as long as everyone is messing around with clay."

"Yes, she's happy to believe that a football star like you is interested in sculpture," Laurie teased. "She'd be so crushed to find out you only took her course because Bob Green told you it was easy."

Chuck laughed. "Yeah, but she'll never know that." He glanced up and waved to a group of boys in an old Plymouth that was pulling out of the school's parking lot. Shaking his head, he said, "Boy, you'd think Mike would be embarrassed to let anyone see him driving that thing."

Laurie didn't reply. Didn't Chuck realize that if she ever could afford any kind of car, she'd be lucky if it looked as good as Mike's? She wished Chuck wouldn't put down someone who'd had to earn the money to buy his own. As she climbed into Chuck's shiny black Jeep she wondered how he would have handled it if his dad hadn't bought him the car he wanted.

Very soon the Jeep was parked in front of Pop's Pizza and Laurie and Chuck were settled at a table in the front window. It was kind of dumb to drive there from school—after all, Laurie thought, we could walk here almost faster than driving—but there was something wonderful about being able to go wherever you wanted without waiting for an adult to drive. It made it even better, Laurie admitted to herself, that it was Chuck Stillwell's car she'd been riding in for the last couple of weeks.

Laurie watched as Chuck went back to the counter for another slice of pizza. She still couldn't believe he liked her, wanted to spend time with her rather than some other, more popular girl. Chuck could have been a model for the perfect all-American guy: Tall, broad-shouldered, and strong, with sandy-blond hair and brilliant blue eyes. A smile tugged at the corners of his mouth nearly all the time—Chuck didn't seem to take anything very seriously.

Watching Chuck as he stood waiting for his pizza and kidding with the woman behind the counter, Laurie thought how lucky she was to be dating such a good-looking guy. Well, sort of dating—Chuck was so busy with football practice every afternoon and games every weekend that they'd never had time to go to the movies or anything like that. But he'd asked her to come to the party after last Saturday's game and he'd spent the whole evening with her.

It really was amazing how things happened, Laurie thought. She'd hardly ever even spoken to Chuck until about two weeks ago, but of course she'd known who he was. Until recently he'd been going out with Meryl Worthing and everyone had thought of them as the perfect couple. Meryl's gorgeous figure and perfectly groomed blond hair were the envy of every girl in school. Laurie wasn't sure why they'd broken up, and at the moment she didn't care.

As Laurie's gaze strayed across the room crowded with students wolfing down pizza and sodas, she caught sight of her own reflection in the mirrored wall behind the tables. Automatically she pushed back the shiny dark hair that had fallen across her cheek. It definitely wasn't blond like Meryl Worthing's, with every strand knowing its proper place.

Suddenly her wide-set brown eyes gleamed with pleasure as she saw Chuck's reflected image move toward their table. She turned to smile at him as he sat down.

"It's late practice day for the varsity, so I'll be done at seven-thirty," he told her. "You can hang around and watch or something, and then I'll drive you home."

Laurie started to nod in agreement, but then stopped herself—there was a meeting of the school newspaper staff. "Oh, Chuck, I can't," she said regretfully. "I've got to work at the *Pryer* this afternoon—we're trying to get the first issue ready. And then I've got to go home and study. All this chemistry on top of Mr. Gordon's history class—" Laurie sighed.

"Yeah," Chuck said, wiping pizza off his chin. "Only the beginning of October, and already the guy is loading on the work. Seems like there's some kind of assignment every night, and meantime he expects us to be gearing up for the big test on the thirtieth."

Laurie looked at her watch. "We should be getting back," she told Chuck, and then went on, "I guess everyone who said Mr. Gordon's class was the hardest one in this high school was right."

Chuck didn't respond to her comment until they were in the Jeep heading back to school. Then he said, "I don't know, Laurie. Football practice is so demanding, I just can't make time for all this Mickey Mouse homework. But if I start messing up this class, my dad says I'll have to quit the team. It's a problem." He glanced over at Laurie and after a pause added, "Hey, I know how we can solve it. I'll pick you up every morning and you can give me your homework—I'll get it back to you before class."

Laurie looked at him in amazement. Was he serious? Did he really think he could copy her history homework every day? At last she said with an attempt at humor, "Oh, I don't think that would work out, Chuck—I can barely get the history assignment done myself before I sit down in Mr. Gordon's room."

Chuck gave a quick smile. "Hey, just kidding. I guess we'll both be there plugging away at the last minute."

Laurie nodded, but somehow she couldn't think of anything else to say, and they rode the rest of the way to school in silence.

The substitute teacher in math took attendance and then told the class to use the period as a study hall. Laurie started on the math assignment, but it was hard to keep her mind focused. Determined not to think about Chuck's suggestion for cheating on the history homework, she nevertheless couldn't stop his words from replaying in her mind. It must have been a joke. But deep down she knew he had been serious. And what had she said back to him? She couldn't even remember, she'd been so taken by surprise. Another nagging thought floated into her brain. Was Chuck mad at her now?

With a sigh, Laurie opened her math book and looked at the first problem. As she stared at the numbers in their neat rows, suddenly they seemed to go in and out of focus. Frowning, she squinted hard. But her head felt strange—there was a muffled roaring sound in her ears. For a moment she felt as if a giant fishbowl had been inverted over her head, skewing her vision. And then she heard it again—the voice that had cried out during the night. "Please, help me!"

Laurie's head jerked up and she looked around in a panic. No one else seemed to have heard anything—the heads of her classmates were bent over their books. Involuntarily she turned toward the windows at the back of the classroom. Could a child be outside? But no, if a child were crying out there, Laurie would still be hearing him.

With heavy certainty Laurie knew that it was the same voice that had awakened her the night before. And she was still convinced it wasn't something she'd imagined—it was too real for that. Yet how could it be real?

An insistent memory was tugging at the corner of her mind. She didn't want to look at it, but finally she couldn't keep it out. It was the memory of another voice in the middle of the night—another childish cry for help, but that time with choking sounds and splashes like water in the background.

It had sounded like a little kid, maybe four or five years old—the same age as Carlos Weber, the boy she baby-sat for. Laurie had been sound asleep when the voice called out piteously for help. Sitting up and straining to hear it again, she'd been convinced that a young child was drowning somewhere. In fact, she'd been so certain that she'd gotten up and dressed.

Taking a flashlight, she'd hurried to the park a block away where she often took Carlos to play. A stream ran down and formed a small pond at the bottom of the park, and Laurie had approached it fearfully, yet with an urgent need to find the child who was in danger. But no child had been there.

Impatiently Laurie brushed her hair out of her eyes. That was all in the past. It had happened the year Laurie was thirteen—the year her parents split up. The three of them had been through a miserable time full of hateful anger and even more awful silences. Laurie had read a lot since then about how divorce affects a family, and she recognized all the symptoms—

the feeling that the divorce was somehow her fault, the anger and confusion about what was going on, the sense of being alone and excluded from the decisions that would change her life as much as anyone else's.

Well, thank goodness that was all over. But now the memory of another voice intruded. It was soon after she and her dad had moved to the new house.

She had been home alone one afternoon. It was a gloomy day and Laurie felt a little strange. She decided to turn on some lights to cheer up the house that didn't contain much furniture yet. As she reached for the light switch in the kitchen, she heard someone weeping in despair.

"Oh, what's the use, I can't stand this anymore! I can't go on, I'd be better off dead." Laurie turned cold—it was her mother's voice. The broken words were hard to make out between the bitter sobs, but Laurie had no doubt that it was her mom.

With shaking hands Laurie picked up the phone. As she punched in the still-unfamiliar numbers she silently willed her mother to answer and assure her that everything was fine. But the phone just kept ringing, and after a long time Laurie slowly replaced the receiver.

Mom's out, she told herself. Maybe she went to work today. You were just imagining things. Just go do your homework and quit worrying.

But she couldn't. The words kept repeating over and over in her mind and she flinched every time they hammered again—"better off dead, better off dead, better off dead."

Laurie put her hands over her ears, but she couldn't block out the voice. Was her mom really out somewhere or was she at her apartment, so full of despair that she couldn't make herself answer the phone? Had she flung herself down on her bed in a flood of tears? Though Laurie tried to banish it, the terrifying question kept sneaking into her head. Had her mom felt so hopeless that she'd tried to kill herself?

Grabbing her purse, Laurie raced out the door and down the narrow street. It was nearly half a mile to the bus stop and her breath was coming in gasps when she reached it. The first bus to pull up was going to the wrong destination, and Laurie waited in feverish impatience until at last the right one arrived.

Her mother's new apartment was only a few miles from where Laurie and her father lived, but the bus driver seemed to be going as slowly as he possibly could, coasting to every intersection to catch the red light. By the time she got off, Laurie's fingers were cramped from clutching the grab bar. As she flew along the sidewalk scraps of thoughts tumbled in her brain. If her mom didn't answer the door, Laurie would find someone with a key to let her in—surely there must be a manager or a superintendent or someone like that. She'd just have to convince them it was important and—

Laurie yanked open the outside door of the small apartment building and stood panting in front of the panel of buzzers. Which one was her mom's? There it was, the third one down on the left. She held it down hard. Come on, Mom, answer the door, please be there, please be all right—

"Who is it?"

Laurie's throat was dry and she had to swallow hard before she could reply. Trembling with relief, she said, "Mom? It's me, Laurie. Can I come up?"

There was a pause, and then Laurie could hear the surprise in her mother's voice. "Of course, honey. I'll buzz you in."

Standing in the doorway of her apartment, Laurie's mother looked puzzled. "I didn't expect to see you today," she said in a questioning tone.

"Well," Laurie began awkwardly, "I just felt like seeing you. I wanted to make sure you were okay." Even before she saw her mom's eyebrows go up, Laurie knew it sounded strange. But what else could she say?

A raucous sound made Laurie jump. It was the buzzer signaling the end of sixth period. All around her people were gathering up their books and heading for the door. She shook her head, trying to clear away the fog of memories that had engulfed her.

Closing her math book with a thump, Laurie thought, I didn't get much done in this class. I'd better get myself in gear—there's still English and French to get through before the end of the day.

CHAPTER 3

LAURIE JOINED IN THE CHORUS OF SIGHS and groans as Madame Engelke announced a surprise quiz in French class. When at last the bell rang, Laurie handed in her paper and headed out into the corridor to her locker. Amy Roberts was waiting there for her.

"What a day!" Amy gestured at the heap of books and notebooks on the floor beside her. "I swear, I think every single one of these teachers thinks we're a bunch of lazy you-know-whats and they all got together and decided this was the week to show us how hard junior year is going to be. There's even an assignment for health tonight!"

Laurie nodded in agreement. "I know," she told her friend. "I'm feeling kind of snowed under and it's only the fifth of October. But listen, Amy, I have to go to the library and—"

"Oh, me, too," Amy broke in. "I want to look at some of those books for the history research project before everyone else takes them out."

"Yeah, that's what I was thinking," Laurie

said. With her stack of books balanced precariously in her arms, she stood up and slammed the locker shut with one foot, then carefully reached one hand out to twist the combination lock. "Although I don't see how I can possibly carry any more books home than I've already got here," she added with a laugh.

"Oh, come on, Laurie, you don't have to worry about that," Amy said in a teasing voice as they started down the hall. "From what I can tell, you've got someone ready to carry your books whenever you want. Isn't Chuck going to drive you home?"

Laurie shook her head. "Not today—he's got late football practice and I told him I had to go to the *Pryer* meeting and then get home and start working on all this stuff." Laurie's smile faded as she remembered Chuck's suggestion about copying her homework. She still wanted to believe he'd been joking, but the incident seemed to cast a cold shadow across her thoughts.

Laurie pushed the uneasiness out of her mind and turned her attention to her friend's cheerful chatter. Amy was Laurie's opposite in lots of ways—she was short and wiry, and her frizzy blond flyaway hair seemed to crackle with her nonstop energy. At five-foot-five, Laurie certainly didn't think of herself as tall, and it always surprised her that Amy envied her those extra three inches. She smiled to herself. She often wished she had a mop of natural curls like Amy's, but Amy would trade those curls in an instant for what she called Laurie's "gorgeous" straight, dark brown hair.

The two of them had met in ninth grade and had instantly become close friends. Now Amy was talking about the volleyball team.

"So I told her I didn't think I was going to have time to play volleyball this fall, and she gave me this real pathetic look, like I'm-so-disappointed-in-you-Miss-Roberts. But really, Laurie, there are plenty of people trying out for the team, so it's not as if they won't be able to play without me, and I really want to get into working on the *Pryer,* you know? And I just don't know if I can do both and still keep my grades up, which if I don't, my folks are going to be *extremely* upset."

Amy paused for breath, and Laurie said, "Well, you weren't crazy about volleyball last year anyway. So you might as well wait until track season starts and then see if you have time to do any sports."

"Yeah, you're right, that's exactly what I was thinking," Amy said as they pushed open the door to the library.

Plopping their books down on an empty table, the two girls rummaged through their papers. Then, armed with the list of source books from history class, they located the shelf where the books had been put on reserve for Mr. Gordon's students.

"Do you think we'll get extra credit for being

the first ones here?" Amy whispered as they pulled out some of the books.

"Oh, sure, definitely," Laurie replied sarcastically. "No, all we'll get is the chance to choose the least boring of all these to use for this comparison project."

Amy wrinkled her nose. "They all look pretty tedious, don't they?"

An hour later Laurie closed another fat volume and put it back on the shelf. The first book she'd looked at was by far the best, she thought. She looked at her watch. "Hey, Amy, we'd better get over to the *Pryer*."

"Oh, my gosh!" Amy slapped her own book shut. "Okay, I'm ready. This one"—she waved a hand at the book—"is actually not too bad for a history book."

They waited while the librarian found their names on Mr. Gordon's class list and then checked out their books. Gathering up her pile of books and papers, Laurie said, "I need a suitcase to carry all this stuff!"

"A suitcase? No, what we need is a wheelbarrow," Amy told her with a laugh.

The halls were less crowded now, and they hurried along one long corridor and around a corner to the wing where the *Pryer*'s "office" was. The school newspaper came out on an irregular schedule (translated, that meant it came out whenever the staff managed to get an issue ready). Known for its high standards of writing and reporting as well as its humor, the

Pryer was run mostly by seniors. Laurie knew that as juniors, she and Amy were lucky to have a chance to work on it, even though most of what they'd done so far was odd jobs.

The newspaper had been moved this year to half of a former classroom—the other half, behind a temporary partition, was used by the guidance department. Laurie thought it was fortunate that no one was in the guidance office now, because the *Pryer*'s staff was making a lot of noise.

Mark Jacobs, the editor in chief, lounged in a battered wooden armchair that was tilted back at a dangerous angle. Laurie found her eyes drawn to him—with his strong, angular features and deep voice, he was someone whose presence people noticed. His scruffy sneakers rested on an ancient desk between stacks of paper topped with cryptic notes like *Do this by Friday* or *Not ready—needs more R.* Laurie assumed that someone knew what these messages meant, but on the other hand it seemed to her that every time she looked at the papers, the stacks were higher.

Mark was talking to Hilary Jones, the *Pryer*'s second-in-command. At a table against the wall several people were clustered around the one computer terminal, arguing about the best way to get the machine to rearrange some columns. Another group was handing around a set of photographs from Saturday's football game and making loud comments about each picture.

"Hey, it's Amy and Laurie!" Mark swung his long legs off the desk and set down his chair with a crash. "Sounds like a song title, doesn't it? So good, now that you're here, we'll have our traditional editorial meeting." He raised his voice. "Okay, everybody, meeting time! Angela, put down those photos and look alert—and Sean, give the machine a chance to recover while you tell us what's ready and what isn't." He glanced around the group. "Hilary will be taking notes so we'll all know who promised to do what. Remember, this is our first issue this year, so I want it to be a winner."

As the meeting went on, Laurie thought that Mark was the perfect person to be in charge of the newspaper. He obviously expected everyone to work hard, and since he worked hard himself, no one minded. Besides, Mark had good ideas for articles that would really interest the whole school.

They went through the plans for the first issue page by page. Sports, profiles of new teachers, a feature article by Hilary on homelessness in the surrounding community. "I thought we could link that up with Sean's article on what the Key Club is planning for the Thanksgiving dinner they're going to hold for the homeless," Hilary said.

"Good idea," Mark said with enthusiasm. "Let's talk to Mr. Carelli—isn't he in charge of the dinner this year?" When Hilary nodded, Mark went on, "Okay, so someone should talk to him and see if he needs volunteers for the dinner—we could end Sean's piece with a request for volunteers and refer questions to Mr. Carelli if he wants."

"Okay." Hilary scribbled a note on her list. "Now, what about the article on the student government survey?"

"It's not done yet." Angela held up her hands in mock self-defense. "I know, I know, it's supposed to be turned in already, but something got messed up and the surveys didn't get distributed to three of the ninth-grade homerooms."

Hilary looked annoyed. "You could have let me know that sooner," she told Angela. "Now we'll have to—um, let's see, if they get them tomorrow—" She looked over at Laurie. "After we're done, take the survey master over to the copy room and make about seventy-five copies. Then you can put twenty-five in each teacher's box whose class didn't fill them out yet—get the names from Angela—and stick on a note to say we need them back by Thursday morning at the latest."

Laurie nodded as Hilary made a check mark on her list. It was lucky for the *Pryer* that Hilary was so organized, she thought, or the first issue wouldn't be out until the end of the term.

When the meeting was over, Angela helped Laurie find the master copy of the survey that had been distributed to each class in the high school. "I don't know what happened," Angela told her. "I was sure every class got the surveys. Anyway, just make enough copies and put them in these teachers' boxes." Handing Laurie a crumpled sheet of paper with three names scrawled on it, Angela turned away. "See you later."

After the non-stop chatter of the *Pryer* office, the copy room was eerily quiet. The only sound was the low hum of the machines. Like many older schools, Granville High School's brick building had been added to over the years, and as more space was needed many rooms had been divided in odd ways. The copy room was one of those that had been carved out of a larger area; it was entered through a short passageway that turned sharply to the right to form a long narrow room. It felt like a secret place hidden away from the normal activity of the school.

The newest copy machine was at the end of the room, and Laurie was pleased to see that no one was using it. She stood in front of it and peered at the various digital readout boxes—every machine seemed to have a different method for selecting the number of copies to be made. Suddenly, behind her, Laurie heard a whispery swishing sound. A shiver ran down her spine and she froze for a moment, then spun around quickly. "Who's there?"

"Oh!" The girl who stood up from behind the other large copy machine looked almost frightened by Laurie's words. "Um, well, um, hi, Laurie."

"Oh, Millie, I didn't know anyone was here." Laurie grinned sheepishly at the other girl. "You startled me. Were you hiding?"

"Gosh, I'm sorry," Millie said. A hot red flush spread over her face and she turned away, ducking her head so that Laurie could hardly hear her next words. "No, I wasn't hiding, I was trying to load new paper in the machine and I just can't get it to work."

"Don't you just hate when that happens?" Laurie said cheerfully. "Want some help?"

Without waiting for an answer, Laurie walked over and squatted down to tug at the paper tray. It resisted for a moment and then finally slid out to its open position. Laurie held the clamps open and watched as Millie carefully loaded in a large stack of paper. Her hands were trembling so much that the top sheet of each new batch of paper was knocked askew.

The silence between the two girls was beginning to feel a little awkward. In a determinedly chatty tone Laurie asked, "What are you making so many copies of, anyway?"

Millie blushed again as she answered, "I think it's a reading list for ninth-grade English. I, um, work for Ms. Moreson in the high-school office and I do a lot of copying for her."

Laurie pushed the paper tray closed and stood up. "Oh, really? You mean it's a paying job?" When the younger girl nodded, Laurie said, "Sounds great."

Returning to the other machine, she soon had the various knobs and dials set. In what seemed like only a few seconds the machine had spit out her seventy-five copies of the survey. Laurie gathered up the papers. "Bye, Millie, see you."

Walking down the hall to deliver the surveys to the high-school office, Laurie thought, Poor Millie—if she blushes when she has to talk to me, she must have heart failure if she ever has to say anything in a class. Laurie had always thought of herself as a shy person, but compared with Millie, she was Miss Congeniality.

She wondered how long Millie had been working for Ms. Moreson. It was unusual for a student to have a paying job at school, especially a tenth grader. I guess she must really need the money, Laurie thought.

Back at the *Pryer* office, everyone was in a mild state of hysteria. Sean shoved some papers into Laurie's hand as soon as she walked in and said, "Richard gave me this profile, but it's much too long! You've got to cut out at least four lines or it will never fit—and could you proofread it, too, while you're at it? I don't trust Richard's spelling."

Clearing a space for herself on one of the tables, Laurie read through the article and then went back to the beginning. It was hard to figure out what could be dropped from the piece about Ms. Simons, the new teacher in the math department, but Laurie discovered that it was like working a puzzle. Soon she was crossing out a phrase here and half a line there and counting to see whether she had shortened the article enough. Proofreading was the next step; Laurie enjoyed the knowledge that when she finished, the spelling and punctuation in this article would be as perfect as she could make them.

She was only halfway through when Amy peered over her shoulder. "Hey, you found a lot of mistakes—remind me to never ask Richard how to spell anything," Amy said with a laugh. "Listen, Laurie, I'm done, so I'm going to get on home—I have to baby-sit the brats so Mom can go to some meeting, and I have a *lot* of homework to do." She crammed one more book into her bookbag and swung it to her shoulder. "See you tomorrow, okay?"

"Yeah, see you," Laurie replied, and then turned her attention once more to the papers in front of her.

When at last she had finished, Laurie lifted her head and was surprised to see that almost everyone had left. Only Sean still sat in front of the word processor, grumbling to himself occasionally as his fingers tapped out the letters.

Laurie handed him the pages she'd marked up. "Here's Richard's article, Sean," she told him. "I think it should fit now. I managed to cut about four and a half lines."

"Excellent!" Sean brushed a hand across his

tight curls as if he expected to find a bird nesting there—Laurie had seen him make this gesture hundreds of times. "And it looks like you did a great job of proofreading. Maybe I'll make you my assistant so I don't have to check all this stuff myself."

Laurie smiled. "Fine with me," she told him. "Actually it's kind of fun."

Collecting her books, Laurie walked to the door. "Bye, Sean, see you tomorrow," she called.

Without turning his head, Sean muttered, "Yeah, okay, bye."

The corridor was silent as Laurie walked toward the entrance to the high school. Emptied of the noisy crowds that filled the halls during the day, it felt eerie, almost scary. Laurie caught herself looking back over her shoulder as she hurried along. A low rushing noise filled her ears. And then she heard the voice.

"Help me!"

She could hardly make out the words because of the bitter sobs that muffled them, but Laurie knew it was the same voice she'd heard twice before. She stood motionless in the dim hallway, her hands clammy and her heart pounding. But the voice didn't come again.

CHAPTER 4

"HELLO, HELLO! LAURIE, YOU HOME?"

"Hi, Dad," Laurie called, getting up from the desk in her room and walking out to the head of the stairs. She glanced at her watch: 6:30. "You're home early."

"Yes, but I've got to go out again in an hour or so." Laurie's father spoke in a loud voice as he picked up the mail and riffled through it. "I brought Chinese food for a change."

"Oh, good." They'd had Chinese food over the weekend and today was only Monday, but Laurie knew there was no point in mentioning it. Her dad was always so busy and he tried hard to find time to spend with his only child. In turn, Laurie tried hard not to cause more problems for him than he already had to deal with. His small real-estate business was fairly successful, but only because he put in such long hours.

She went back into her room to finish the notes she'd been making when he arrived. Then she clattered down the shiny wooden staircase and scooped up the bag of food. "Mm, smells good," she said.

In the kitchen she emptied the shopping bag, lining up all the little white cardboard boxes on the counter. If her dad had to go out again, he'd want to eat right away, she thought. Efficiently she opened the cartons, dumped their contents into microwave-proof serving dishes, and put them in to reheat. Meanwhile she set the table for the two of them. It was next to a floor-to-ceiling window overlooking the hillside full of tall trees and tangled bushes. In the soft light of early evening, Laurie could see a mass of leaves just tinged with the yellow of autumn.

When they sat down to eat, Laurie's father said as he always did, "Well, honey, what's new at Granville High School?"

"Nothing much," she answered as she always did. Then she added, "I was working on the *Pryer* this afternoon—I think it's going to be a lot of fun."

"Good!" Without saying anything more, Laurie's dad helped himself to chicken with black-bean sauce. Laurie wondered if something was wrong. He usually kept up a steady stream of talk while they ate.

At last he looked at Laurie and said heavily, "Your mother called today."

Laurie nodded in silence. So that was it. She waited, her shoulders stiff with tension, as he went on.

"She wants you to come for a visit some

weekend—says she hasn't seen much of you lately."

Laurie let her breath out slowly. "Yeah, okay. I'll call her and work out a date." She looked at her father. "How is she doing?"

"Oh, fine, I guess," he replied. "She seems fine. Say, did you have some of these noodles? They're pretty good."

They talked about other things and then washed the dishes to the accompaniment of a news show on TV. Laurie's father gathered up his papers and stuffed them into his briefcase. "I won't be too late, honey. See you later."

Laurie listened as the front door closed and her dad's car started on the driveway outside. Then she turned to trudge back up the stairs to her room and the homework that was waiting for her. She'd call her mom soon and arrange a weekend visit.

It was strange how Dad still seemed so uncomfortable talking about anything to do with Mom, Laurie thought. After all, they'd been married to each other for a long time—more than fifteen years—so you'd think he wouldn't get so unglued and awkward. Be fair, though, she told herself. You feel awkward and strange with her, too. Maybe people always felt weird if someone they loved had a "nervous breakdown" or "an episode" or whatever the doctors decided to call it.

Laurie knew that her mother had been seeing a therapist—a "shrink," in the language of

Laurie's friends—for a long time. She also knew that her dad didn't really approve of shrinks. He thought people should be strong enough to solve their own problems. He had never actually said so, but Laurie was certain he thought her mother was weak and self-indulgent and that all she needed was to make up her mind to get her life organized. Laurie wasn't so sure he was right, but it was something they rarely talked about.

Casey stretched up on his hind legs and kneaded Laurie's leg with his claws—his way of saying he wanted some attention. She picked up a raveled piece of yarn from the back of her desk and dangled the end of it over his head, smiling as he batted it and then caught it in his mouth.

Laurie smiled at him fondly. Though he was five years old now, Casey still acted like a kitten now and then. Laurie was glad she'd finally succeeded in convincing her parents that she needed a cat. Casey had been there through the whole divorce and the horrible time that had led up to it, and Laurie had been grateful for his comforting presence and his unconditional attachment to her.

She still didn't understand what had caused Mom's breakdown. Was it the reality of knowing that she was divorced and on her own that she hadn't been able to handle? Or was it something else—something to do with Laurie?

Laurie remembered the months before her

parents split up. She hadn't helped things much. She and her mom had fought a lot—arguments that ended in long sulky silences and a feeling that an unbridgeable chasm separated the two of them. Of course, Laurie had been twelve then and all her friends thought their parents didn't understand them either—it was probably the well-known early-adolescent madness everyone wrote about. Still, she couldn't help feeling that if she'd just been a little bit nicer, Mom's problems wouldn't have gotten so bad.

Suddenly Laurie realized that she'd forgotten to call her mom to set up a date to visit her. Glancing at the clock, she thought, It's too late to call her tonight, but I'll do it tomorrow. Now I'd better get moving or this homework will never be done.

At midnight Laurie closed her books and fell wearily into bed. But suddenly she was wide-awake. She turned onto her other side, but she couldn't seem to get comfortable. Leaning on her elbow, she tried scrunching the pillow to a different position. Casey gave her an indignant mew and removed himself to the floor. What's the matter with you? she asked herself in silent irritation. Just close your eyes and relax.

As she lay there, willing herself to drift into sleep, Laurie's head began to feel as if it were held in a vise that was slowly tightening. Then she heard the faint voice calling once again, and she knew it was what she'd been waiting for.

"Oh, please, somebody help me!"

Laurie sat up, straining her ears to hear but the little voice had fallen silent. Where are you? she thought in frustration. Who are you, and why are you calling out to me?

After what seemed a long time, she realized she wouldn't hear it again and fell back against the pillows. As she waited for sleep Laurie wondered miserably, had the voice been real or was it all in her mind?

The next day and the day after that, Laurie went to her classes and did all the normal things she always did. On the outside she knew she looked fine, but inside she couldn't get the voice out of her head. It was becoming an obsession, she thought, and when it woke her again on Wednesday night, she couldn't keep herself from bursting into tears. It sounded so real, and yet she didn't see how it could be a real child's voice. Was she hallucinating? she wondered fearfully. Then, unwillingly, she thought, Am I going crazy, like Mom?

Thursday at lunch she sat with Chuck at their usual table in Pop's Pizza. Gazing out the window, she saw a little boy about five years old. She stared at him, knowing it was absurd to wonder if that could be the child whose voice she kept hearing. Then gradually she became aware of a different voice. "Laurie? Did you hear anything I said?" Chuck sounded really angry.

"Oh, Chuck, I'm sorry." She felt herself blushing and hurried on. "I was listening, but—it's just that I—" She stopped abruptly and then started over. "Really, I'm sorry. What were you saying?"

Still obviously annoyed, Chuck shrugged his shoulders. "Nothing important," he said shortly. "But I don't know what's with you, Laurie. You seem like you're on another planet sometimes."

"Sometimes I'd like to be," Laurie told him lightly, but her attempt at a joke fell flat. And then all of a sudden, before she'd really made up her mind about telling him, the whole story came pouring out—the voice, her own fears, her frustration at not understanding what was happening.

When she stopped talking, Chuck looked at her in amazement. "You're hearing voices in the middle of the night? Some little kid is calling you for help and you don't know who it is?"

When Laurie nodded, a mischievous grin spread across Chuck's face. "Hoo, boy, that's plenty weird." He shook his head. "Either this is the biggest joke of all time . . ." He gave Laurie a questioning look.

"It's not a joke, Chuck," she said slowly.

He laughed out loud. "I don't know, Laurie. Maybe you should think about going into business as a whatchamacallit—a medium. You could probably make a fortune around this town communicating with people's long-lost relatives. Hey, better yet, do you think you can predict what number will win the lottery?" Still chuckling, he stood up and motioned for Laurie to precede him out the door. "My little gypsy fortune-teller. Boy, I can't wait to hear who else talks to you in the middle of the night."

Laurie said nothing. What had possessed her to tell Chuck about the voice she kept hearing? Now he thought she was either lying or crazy—he obviously hadn't even considered the possibility that the voice was real. In a panic Laurie thought, Is he going to tell all his friends? I don't think I could stand it.

As Chuck steered his Jeep into the school parking lot, Laurie said, trying hard to keep her voice calm, "Chuck, I'd rather you didn't tell anyone else about what I told you. Actually I'd just like to forget all about it."

"Yeah, I bet you would." Chuck laughed again. He parked the car neatly and then turned to Laurie, placing one hand dramatically over his heart. "Your secret is safe with me, Laurie." His voice was artificially deep, like an old-time radio announcer, and Laurie knew he was making fun of her. But at least he had promised not to tell.

"Okay. Thanks," she told him. As they walked into the school building they joined a group of their classmates returning from lunch, and Chuck got caught up in an ongoing argument about the Giants' chances of making it to the Super Bowl. He didn't seem to hear Laurie when she said, "See you later, Chuck," and went down the corridor toward her locker.

It was hard for her to focus on her classes that afternoon. The scene with Chuck kept unrolling in her mind's eye, and each time she felt the same humiliation as she remembered how he'd laughed at her story. He must think I'm a total idiot, she thought miserably. Why did I open my stupid mouth and tell him about it?

Laurie could barely smile at Amy when she arrived at the *Pryer* office, but soon she was swept up in a series of jobs that all had to be done right away. She felt almost cheerful as she sped along the hall with a bunch of notices to put in teachers' boxes in the high-school office. Pushing open the door, she greeted Ms. Moreson, the school secretary, and then turned toward the honeycomb wall of mailboxes.

Laurie froze, her hand stretching out absurdly in front of her with a paper clutched in it. Chuck was standing by the window, his head bent close as he talked quietly to a slim girl with light brown hair—Millie Banks. Laurie noticed without wanting to that Millie was really very pretty when she smiled.

With an effort Laurie started walking again toward the boxes on the wall. "Hi, Chuck—hi, Millie," she said brightly.

As Chuck turned to look over his shoulder Millie blushed and looked terrified. For heaven's sake, Laurie thought with irritation, does she think I'm going to start a fight with her or something?

Chuck raised a hand in greeting. "Hey, Laurie." His voice was casual—almost too casual, Laurie thought. Then he turned his attention back to Millie.

Hurt, Laurie faced the wall of mailboxes and began putting one of the papers into each little cubbyhole. As she stretched on tiptoe to reach the top row of boxes, some of the papers clutched in her left hand slipped from her grasp and slid to the floor. Suppressing the urge to stamp her foot in frustration, she knelt to pick them up carefully, hoping they hadn't gotten too smudged with dirt. She patted the remaining papers back into a neater pile and started to stand up.

"Here, let me help you with that." She looked up quickly, relieved to hear the familiar warmth back in Chuck's voice. But he was taking a large box out of Millie's arms.

"It's okay, you don't have to—" Millie spoke so softly that Laurie could hardly hear her.

"No, it's much too heavy for you, and I'm walking down that way anyway," Chuck interrupted cheerfully. "You just open the doors for me and tell me where to put this stuff when we get there."

As he reached the door of the office Chuck glanced back at Laurie. "See you tomorrow."

Laurie stared after him as he followed Millie

out into the corridor. As the door clicked shut she wondered miserably, Is Chuck mad at me? Or does he think I'm crazy, hearing voices that aren't really there?

CHAPTER 5

THE NEXT DAY WAS FRIDAY. BUT AT least it's not Friday the thirteenth, Laurie thought as she hurried through the main doors of Granville High School. That must be a good sign. In the lobby full of students rushing into the office or sauntering toward the classrooms, she glanced around for Chuck. Often he waited for her near the doors and walked her to her first class, but today he was nowhere in sight. Never mind, she told herself. I'll see him in history second period.

Still, she hung around the lobby for a few more minutes and then had to race to get to health class on time. Sliding into her seat just as the buzzer sounded, she dumped her books on the floor and quickly stood up again for the Pledge of Allegiance.

The day's announcements came over the PA system—French-club meeting, extra band rehearsal, score of yesterday's soccer game (Granville 2–Scottstown 1). Then Laurie jerked to attention as the disembodied voice of Allen

Baumbusch, student council president, got louder and full of enthusiasm. "And don't forget, tonight is the varsity football team's date with destiny—the big game against Millbrook! This is an away game so get yourselves to the Millbrook football field by seven o'clock and prepare to cheer our Panthers on to victory! See you there!"

As Ms. Jenkins started to collect the health homework, Laurie began making a mental list of people who might be driving to the game at Millbrook. Opening her textbook, she thought, I'll ask Chuck if he knows who's going to be there. Then I can talk to someone about a ride to the game.

Laurie was almost the first one out the door when the bell rang at the end of class. She stood in the corridor for a moment, scanning the faces that hurried past her in both directions. At last she saw Chuck walking toward her. He was deep in conversation with Jim DeCicca, one of his teammates on the Panthers, and glanced quickly at Laurie as he approached.

"Hey, Laurie, let's go, we're gonna be late," Chuck said impatiently. Still talking about some football player Laurie had never heard of, he strode ahead with Jim. Walking behind them, Laurie felt like a little girl struggling to keep up with the bigger, older kids. It wasn't a very pleasant feeling, and Laurie was glad to reach Mr. Gordon's classroom and make her way to her seat on the other side of the room from Chuck.

She thought she wouldn't be able to keep her mind on American history, but as soon as Mr. Gordon started talking, Laurie found herself fascinated. Mr. Gordon treated his students almost like adults, never talking down to them or simplifying his ideas. It was hard to keep up with his rapid style of speaking, and often even harder to keep up with all the information and questions he threw at them, but Laurie had to admit his class was never dull. Right now he was talking about the events that led up to the American Revolution.

"And so, looking at it from the British point of view, what in the world was wrong with imposing taxes on British subjects whether they lived in London or three thousand miles away in the colonies? And why shouldn't those colonists who were instigating riots be put down by soldiers with guns? After all, that's what happens in the United States today when people start riots in the cities."

Mr. Gordon paused for a moment and looked at the students to see the effect of his words. Then he went on, "There are always at least two sides to every question, in history and in today's world. And people who are too stubborn or too stupid to try to understand someone else's point of view cause more trouble in the world than all the thugs and criminals put together. No one says you have to accept the other guy's point of view—just make an effort to understand what it is."

"But, Mr. Gordon—" It was Richard Stevens, the *Pryer* reporter whose article on the new math teacher Laurie had proofread on Monday. Laurie didn't know him very well—their schedules had rarely overlapped until this year—but she did know he loved to argue. "What about all the situations where one side of the issue is right and the other is just plain wrong? I mean, what about Nazis or the Ku Klux Klan or something? Their point of view is completely wrong as far as most people are concerned in this day and age, so what would be the point of trying to understand their angle on things?"

"Well, what about it?" Mr. Gordon looked around the room. "No one has any thoughts on Richard's question? Let's follow his reasoning to its logical conclusion. If we don't have to bother understanding the ideas and viewpoints of people like Hitler, how are we going to deal with them? Shoot them? Lock them up? On the other hand, are there any benefits we might predict from attempting to understand their point of view?"

The room was silent for a few moments. Then Laurie, who almost never spoke up in class, was amazed to find her hand in the air. When Mr. Gordon nodded in her direction, she said, "Maybe by trying to understand an opposing point of view, people can figure out how to compromise or settle their problems without always starting wars about everything."

"Oh, sure," Richard told her sarcastically, "psychology's gonna save the world, right?"

"Well, why not give it a try?" Hannah Green's eyes were alight with enthusiasm. "I think Laurie's right, the only way to stop people fighting all the time is to make them get to understand each other. And if we don't use psychology or whatever you want to call it, we're just wasting the information we've got."

As the discussion went on Laurie found she was passionately defending the idea of doing psychological research to discover what made some people use violence to get their way while others try to persuade or convince the rest of the world that their ideas are right. Richard continued to insist that some ideas were right while others were wrong, and that it was silly to try to understand wrong ideas. Laurie wasn't sure he was completely serious, because he seemed to be having a lot of fun, but then she realized that she was enjoying the discussion, too.

"All right," Mr. Gordon said at last with a look at the clock, "let's get back to the colonists and their disagreement with England. We've been looking at the events that led up to the Revolution from the colonists' point of view up to now. For this weekend's assignment, I want you to examine one of those events from the English point of view. Write three-to-five pages to explain why the English thought and acted as they did in a particular situation."

The buzzer sounded and Laurie gathered up her books amid a chorus of groans.

"Three-to-five pages! Is he kidding?"

"I've got to write a paper for English *and* do two days' worth of math. I can't believe it!"

"Another paper? I'll never survive this class."

As Laurie reached the door she heard Chuck's voice behind her. "Hey, Laurie, that psychology stuff is just your style, right? I bet you knew what the assignment was before Mr. G said a word."

Laurie whirled to face him, but what could she say? Chuck was laughing at her expression. "Just a joke, Laurie, take it easy," he told her. He walked along the hall with her and then stopped where another corridor branched off toward the art and sculpture rooms. "Listen, Laurie, I hope you weren't planning to come to the game tonight." Laurie stared at him. What did he mean?

"Because I don't think it's worth it," Chuck went on. "It looks like it might rain, so the game might be canceled, and then afterward I've got some stuff I've got to do."

"Okay." Laurie's voice sounded strangled to her ears but obviously Chuck heard her.

"Yeah, well, I'll give you a call over the weekend, okay?" Without waiting for her reply, Chuck turned away and strode off down the hall, and Laurie could hear him calling cheerfully to a friend.

At lunchtime Laurie found Amy and the two of them walked to the deli, then brought their sandwiches back and sat on the lawn in front of the school to eat them. The weather was still warm, but the air felt heavy and full of electricity. "I bet the game tonight gets canceled," Amy said through a mouthful of salami and cheese.

Laurie nodded, then took a deep breath and told her friend, "I wasn't going to go anyway, Chuck has something he has to do afterward."

Surprised, Amy looked questioningly at Laurie. But before she could say anything, Richard Stevens dropped down on the grass beside them. "So, Laurie, are you going to try to understand my point of view or should I try to understand yours?" His kidding was directed at Laurie, but she noticed that his eyes and his smile were focused on Amy. And as the three of them sat there talking, Laurie felt more and more left out.

The rest of the day dragged on slowly, and when it was finally over, Laurie couldn't wait to get home and be by herself. It didn't help at all that as she was hurrying from English class to French, her last class of the day, she saw Chuck standing in the hallway talking to Millie Banks, his tall form angled to bring his head close to hers.

The wind was rising, and Laurie felt the first fat raindrops on her head and arms as she turned the key in the lock of her front door. She stepped inside, and the sky seemed to darken suddenly, making the house feel gloomy and oppressive. In a moment the rain was coming down hard, enclosing the house in a gray curtain that was impossible to see through. Laurie checked to make sure all the windows were closed and then climbed the stairs to her room. Through the window she saw a jagged bolt of lightning angle through the sky, its brilliant light piercing the sheets of rain.

Casey stared at Laurie from the middle of her bed. His ears were pulled back against his head and his expression looked a little wild—Casey didn't like storms. Laurie dropped down beside him and gathered him into her lap, stroking his smooth fur hard until he started to purr. And then the lights went out.

They flickered on again after only a few seconds, but it was long enough for Laurie to realize how cut off from the world she was in this lonely house. The idea was scary, but also oddly appealing. It might be nice, she thought, if I never had to talk to or care about anyone again.

Then she shook her head angrily. Cut it out, she told herself, you're getting weird. Leaving Casey on the bed with a final pat, Laurie went to her desk and dumped her books and notebooks out of her bookbag. Might as well get started on the homework—better than sitting there feeling sorry for myself. But it was hard to concentrate and Laurie found herself gazing out the window, watching the wind lash and toss the branches.

Sometime later the phone rang. Laurie's father's voice came through with a lot of static. "Hi, honey, everything okay?" When Laurie assured him she was fine, he went on, "I tried to call a while ago, but the lines must have been down somewhere. This is some storm. Anyway, just wanted to tell you I won't be back till late—I'm stuck up here in River Bluffs and the road's flooded, so I'll have to wait awhile. You'll be okay?"

"Sure, Dad," Laurie said. "Don't worry about me, I'm fine. Just stay where you are until the storm lets up. Don't try to drive in it, all right?"

"All right, honey. See you later."

As Laurie hung up the phone she thought, I probably should be annoyed that Dad calls to check on me as if I were a little kid—but actually I kind of like it. She turned back to her books, determined to immerse herself in the chemistry assignment, but instead she stared at the sheets of rain outside the window. She guessed she was lucky—her dad was a nice guy—but she wished she could talk to him about important things. Like right now, it would be good to be able to pour out her confusion and hurt feelings to someone who wasn't part of school life. But she could just hear what her dad would say if she started telling him about Chuck: "Don't worry, honey, things will work out."

A cracking sound startled Laurie, and she looked at the big maple tree in time to see a large branch split away from it and fall slowly to the ground. Laurie shivered—it would be really scary to be outside in this wild weather.

She wasn't sure how much longer she'd been working when she suddenly noticed a lull in the storm. The rain was heavy still but quieter, and the lightning and thunder had moved farther off. Through the drumming of the rain on the roof over her head, Laurie heard the sad little voice she dreaded.

"Oh, please, why doesn't someone come?"

Frozen, Laurie stared with unseeing eyes out the window and her pen dropped from her fingers. Who was this child? And why did he keep calling to her?

But the voice didn't cry out again, and after a while Laurie forced herself to move. Think about something else, she instructed her mind. Do something else—talk to somebody.

Still moving stiffly, Laurie picked up the phone to call Amy. But there was no dial tone. Once again she was alone, cut off from the world.

Determined to keep busy, Laurie went downstairs. She put cat food in Casey's dish and made a sandwich for herself. Turning on the television in the den, she sat and watched news updates about the storm while she ate.

She sat for a while staring at an old movie on cable. When she realized she wasn't even following the plot, Laurie turned off the TV and went reluctantly back upstairs. Sitting at her desk, she tried to concentrate on studying, but her mind just wouldn't obey her. She drifted away from her history book, wondering what Chuck had to do after the game that was so important. And since the game must have been canceled, what was he doing instead? When she looked back guiltily at her book, she discovered she was still on the first page of the chapter.

The wind had risen again, and its eerie howling set Laurie's nerves on edge. The rain rattled against the windows, first louder, then softer, in an irregular pattern. Then, as the wind slackened, Laurie heard a banging noise. Was someone trying to get into the house? Her heart pounded in her chest. What should she do?

The noise came again, louder than before. Laurie took a deep breath. There was no use hiding in her room, she had to find out what the sound was.

Quietly she crept out into the hall and turned off the light. Then she started down the stairs. At the bottom she flattened herself against the wall—this house had too many windows, it was too easy for someone to see inside.

Moving quickly, Laurie sidled into the living room—the sound had seemed to come from that part of the house. She inched along the wall to the edge of the front window. Steeling herself to face whatever might be out there, she peered through the glass, cupping her hand around her eyes to penetrate the darkness.

At first she couldn't see anything. But then she heard the banging noise again and saw what it was—the lid to someone's garbage can that had blown into the yard and gotten caught in the decking around the front door. As the wind tossed it, it banged between the low wall around the decking and the front of the house.

Laurie let out her breath in a long sigh of relief. But she couldn't make herself go back to studying. *I won't accomplish anything tonight,* she thought. Instead she leafed through the magazines on the coffee table. Curling up on the couch, she began to read an article about a wildlife refuge in Mexico.

A loud ringing made Laurie jump, but then she realized it was the phone. Relieved, she picked it up. "Hello?"

"Oh, Laurie, hi, are you okay? Isn't this storm just amazing?" Amy's voice came clearly over the line, as if there'd been no problems at all.

"Oh, Amy, I'm glad you called." Hearing her friend's voice made Laurie realize how much she'd needed to have some human contact.

"Yeah, my mom and I just got back from the all-night market, you know, the one over on Center Street. We got soaked just running from the car to the store and then back again. And guess who works at the market—Millie Banks!

I was so surprised to see her at the checkout, because most of the other people who work there aren't kids, they're older. And I wouldn't want to work on weekend nights, would you?"

"No, it doesn't sound like much fun," Laurie replied.

Amy paused for a moment, and when she spoke again, it wasn't at her usual mile-a-minute pace. She sounded a bit hesitant as she said, "Laurie, I've got to tell you—I was in town doing some errands with my mom, and when the rain started, we ducked into the diner. And, well—Chuck was there, with Meryl." Amy paused, then hurried on. "I don't know what's going on with you two, but they looked like they were having a great time, and, well, I just thought you should know."

Laurie couldn't think of anything to say for a moment. At last she cleared her throat and said, "Thanks—I guess. I mean, I'm glad you told me, I'd hate to be the last one to know they're back together."

"Oh, I don't know if they really are, but—"

Laurie broke into Amy's words. "Yeah, they are, I'm sure. Chuck was kind of strange today and he told me I shouldn't come to the game—I mean, even if it wasn't canceled. I couldn't figure out why he would say that, but I guess now I know."

"Oh, Laurie, I don't know what to say. I'm really sorry, 'cause I know you like him and he's such a cool guy and all."

"Well . . ." Laurie's mind was a jumble of confused emotions and she couldn't seem to put them in any kind of order. "Listen, Amy, I don't think I can talk about it right now. I need to just think things over—okay?"

"Sure, Laurie, I understand," Amy told her. "But call me later, or tomorrow, if you want to."

Laurie put down the phone and wandered back into the living room. It was strange, but she didn't really feel like crying over Amy's news. I guess I'm not that surprised to hear that Chuck and Meryl are back together, she thought. She's a lot more his type than I am. But why did I ever tell him anything about the voice I keep hearing? How could I have been so stupid? Now Laurie did feel her eyes start to fill with tears. Angrily she brushed them away. Don't worry, dummy, she told herself, he's already forgotten all about you and anything you told him.

In an effort to think about something else, Laurie focused on Millie and what Amy had said about her. It would be hard to have a job you had to go to every Friday night. It wouldn't give you much time for a social life. I guess Millie must really need the money, Laurie thought. Then she remembered seeing Millie talking to Chuck in the office yesterday afternoon. He was probably just practicing his charming manner on anything that happened to be female, she thought bitterly—that and letting me know he wasn't interested in me anymore.

Angry and hurt, Laurie trudged up to her bedroom. Soon she was lying burrowed under the covers, listening to the rain pouring down.

CHAPTER 6

THE WORLD LOOKED WASHED CLEAN and sparkly the next morning, and when Laurie went downstairs, she could see her dad walking around outside. Going out to join him, she found that he'd already dragged the fallen branch to one edge of the driveway. He looked at Laurie and smiled.

"Must have been quite a wind to bring this thing down," he said. "We're lucky it didn't hit the house."

Laurie nodded. She'd been scared enough during the storm without having part of a tree crash through the roof.

Her dad was still talking. "I'll saw this into pieces—when it dries out, we'll use it for firewood. But I can't do it now. I want to check and see if anything else came down, and then I've got to run."

Together they walked around the house. No more big branches had fallen, but there were lots of smaller ones and thousands of leaves scattered everywhere. Feeling virtuous, Laurie told her father, "Don't worry, I'll get this stuff cleaned up. It's such a gorgeous day and it'll be a great excuse for avoiding my homework."

"Thanks, but don't spend all day at it," Mr. Carr told her with a laugh. "Maybe tomorrow you can take another break. We'll go out to Robinson's Orchards and get some cider."

After her dad left, Laurie went upstairs to find her grubbiest jeans, the ones she kept for yard work. The phone rang, and after she'd taken a message for her father, she was about to hang up when she thought, Oh, no, I was supposed to call Mom and I never did. I'd better do that right now.

A wave of guilt washed over Laurie as she waited for her mother to pick up the phone. How could she have forgotten? Then she heard Mom's recorded voice asking her to leave a message at the beep.

"Hi, Mom, it's me. I'm really sorry I didn't call you sooner, but—well, anyway, Dad said you wanted me to come and see you, so call me back and tell me when I should come."

Hanging up, Laurie realized that her message had sounded pretty abrupt and unfriendly. Why couldn't she talk like a normal person to her own mother? As she turned to go down the stairs she wondered if that was why she'd "forgotten" to call Mom.

All weekend Laurie tried to keep as busy as possible. She spent a couple of hours cleaning up the yard and bagging the leaves and small branches to be taken away. After a quick shower she settled down and got a lot of her homework done. That evening Hannah came by in her parents' car and the two of them went to Amy's house to watch *Rebel Without a Cause* on video. They'd never seen it before, and even though the cars and clothes looked old-fashioned, it made all of them cry.

On Sunday Laurie and her dad drove out to the orchard and took a long country walk. It was another beautiful day and the lanes of apple trees were full of families picking red juicy apples and filling their bags. Laurie watched as a small girl impatiently waved her mother and father away and began dragging a sack of apples along the grass. Arm in arm, the child's parents smiled fondly at the determined little figure.

Laurie's father was gazing at the same young family with a wistful expression. Was he remembering times when he and Mom took Laurie apple picking?

"Dad, how's Mom doing? Have you heard from her again?" Laurie was astonished to hear the questions pop out of her mouth. She was usually pretty careful not to bring up the subject of her mother in talking with her dad—it just made him uncomfortable and he never said anything anyway.

Now he looked at Laurie in surprise. "No—why do you ask?"

"Well," Laurie replied slowly, "I called her

yesterday, you know, to set up a time to go see her. But her answering machine was on, so I left a message, but she hasn't called me back. So I wondered . . ." Laurie's voice trailed off. What she meant was, "I was worried about her," but somehow she couldn't say that to her dad.

Dad frowned. After a moment he said, "Well, she probably just forgot to return your call, or she's been busy or something." He paused and then added slowly, "I think she's doing okay, Laurie. She's got to deal with her problems on her own—no one else can do it for her." He put his arm around Laurie's shoulders and gave her a quick squeeze. "Try not to worry. I know that piece of advice isn't easy to follow, but try anyway." He smiled down at her. "Come on, let's go get some cider."

Laurie's homework was already finished—a first, she thought ironically—so when they got home late that afternoon, she tried to think of something else to do. Finally she decided she should go through her closet and get all her summer clothes into the laundry to put away. Then she spent some time brushing Casey's long fur until it shone. As she climbed into bed she thought it had turned out that Chuck's breaking up with her hadn't been all bad—at least she'd gotten a lot done since Friday night.

By the next morning, though, Laurie didn't feel so cheerful. How could Chuck not even have called her to tell her his feelings had changed?

Did he assume she'd just come to school and find out in front of everyone she knew that he and Meryl had resumed their relationship? Laurie couldn't let him see how hurt she was by his behavior.

She was happy to run into Amy outside the building. It gave her a lifeline to hold on to as they walked in. Sure enough, there were Chuck and Meryl in the lobby. Chuck's arm was around the blond girl's shoulders and she leaned against him as she laughed up into his eyes. Laurie felt sure that both of them glanced quickly at her to see her reaction. So she kept talking to Amy, her voice a little bit shrill and her laugh a little too loud, and kept her eyes focused on her friend.

All day it seemed to Laurie that Chuck and Meryl were everywhere she went. She saw them outside the door of Mr. Gordon's room before second period; she saw them in Chuck's Jeep screeching out of the parking lot at lunchtime; she saw them after school walking hand in hand down the hall. What made it even worse was that Amy went for pizza with Richard Stevens at lunchtime, leaving Laurie to find someone else to eat with.

By the end of the day Laurie felt exhausted and irritable. Amy was standing by her locker when Laurie got there to collect her books. "Going to the *Pryer* office, Laurie?" Amy asked cheerfully.

"No, I've got too much work to do, I'm going

home," Laurie snapped. She felt ashamed of herself when she saw Amy's look of hurt surprise, but she didn't try to stop the other girl from leaving.

"Okay, talk to you later," Amy said quickly, and vanished down the hall.

Things were no better on Tuesday, and by the time she got home that afternoon Laurie was feeling that life was definitely unfair. There was no message on the answering machine from her mom and Laurie was sure she knew why. She's probably so mad at me for not calling her sooner that she never wants to have anything to do with me again.

She flung herself down on her bed, not even taking time to pat Casey. Looking extremely cross, he jumped off the bed and walked in a dignified manner out of the room.

I'd like to just leave here and never come back, Laurie thought bleakly. I'm sure everyone's wondering what's wrong with me to make Chuck break up with me after only a few weeks. And I know I've hurt Amy's feelings by not talking to her about anything.

But how can I talk to her? Laurie thought about her friend's bubbly personality and nonstop chatter. She's so happy and cheerful and sane, and I'm so messed up. I *want* to talk to her, about Chuck and about my mom and about the voices, but I'm afraid she'll just laugh at me or decide I'm totally crazy, and I don't think I could stand it.

Sitting up, Laurie stared at her reflection in the mirror over her dresser, and her huge solemn eyes stared back at her. I wonder if I am a little bit crazy, she thought, just like Mom. Maybe the voice *isn't* real. Maybe it's all in my head and it's the first sign of going nuts.

A shiver trickled down Laurie's back and she stared at herself for a moment longer. Then she shook her head and pushed aside a long lock of hair that had fallen across her face. Get it together, Laurie, she told herself. Quit moping around. If you can't cheer up, you can at least do some homework. But as she got out her notebooks and sat down at her desk, she shivered involuntarily again, feeling how alone she was in the silent house.

Laurie still felt sort of like a zombie as she went to her classes the next day and tried to pay attention to what was going on. In history she resolutely kept her eyes away from Chuck and tried not to hear him laughing and joking with a group of his friends.

At lunchtime Amy appeared beside her locker. "Come on, Laurie," she said, taking Laurie's arm and pulling her around so they stood face-to-face. "Let's go get something at the deli—I need to talk to you."

As they sat under a tree and unwrapped their sandwiches, Amy said, "I know it's really too chilly to sit outside, but it's the only place we can talk without everyone hearing every single word we say. Now listen, Laurie, I know you're upset about Chuck, and I'm really sorry, but there's no reason for you to take it out on me and your other friends. And besides, if you're going to go around looking like the world fell in on your head, you're just giving him the satisfaction of seeing how much he matters to you. You've got to show him you don't care about him and stupid Meryl."

Laurie stared at her uneaten sandwich for a moment. Then she looked at Amy. "You're right, I know you are," she said quietly. "But it's not just Chuck that I'm upset about."

When she didn't go on, Amy said, "Well, what is it then?"

But Laurie shook her head. "I can't talk about it, Amy, it's all confused in my mind."

Amy looked searchingly at her friend. With a shrug, she said, "Well, okay. But if you ever do want to talk, you know I'm always here. And meantime I want you to promise me you'll come to the *Pryer* office after school. Everyone's going crazy trying to get the first issue going, and Mark was asking me yesterday where you were. Promise?"

Laurie nodded. With a smile she said, "Yes, Mother, I promise."

"Great!" Amy took a huge bite of her sandwich and then said indistinctly, "Listen, I have to tell you what Madame Engelke said to Jordan this morning."

Amy rattled on, and Laurie thought, I guess it's been pretty obvious that I'm feeling unhappy. But Amy's right, I have to start getting over it.

True to Amy's prediction, the *Pryer* office after school was chaos. Everyone seemed to be working on something totally different, and everyone had to talk to Mark or Hilary or use the computer or get something urgent done right away. When Laurie walked in, Mark greeted her with enthusiasm. "Laurie! I thought you'd given up on us and deserted us forever. Boy, am I glad to see you."

Mark grabbed her arm and steered her to an empty table, where he sat down next to her. Waving a bunch of papers in front of her, he said, "This is Hilary's first draft of the article on homelessness. But it's not in great shape, to put it mildly. Will you look at it and see if you can rewrite it so it'll really make an impact? It's our lead article for the issue, so I want it to be great."

Did Mark think she could fix up the lead article for the paper and make it something exciting to read? Flattered but a bit nervous, Laurie told him, "I'll try."

"Excellent! Come and talk to me when you've gotten some of it done, okay?"

Laurie nodded, and as Mark went to talk to Sean she began to read.

Mark was right—Hilary's first draft had lots of important facts about homelessness in the entire United States and in the area around Granville. But somehow it wasn't very interesting to read. When she'd gone through it twice and made some notes in the margin, Laurie put down her pencil. Staring blankly into space, she thought in frustration, There's something wrong with the whole way this is written.

Five minutes later she jumped as Mark dropped into the chair beside her. "You looked like you were in a trance," he said teasingly. "So I had to wake you up. What do you think?" He gestured at the heap of papers on the desk.

"Well, there's a lot of information in it," she told Mark hesitantly. "But it's—well, it's kind of boring to read."

Mark laughed. "You're absolutely right. Hilary's a great organizer and manager, but she's not exactly the world's greatest writer. Do you think you can fix it up so people will really want to read it?" He paused, then added, "Don't be afraid you'll hurt Hilary's feelings—she's just hoping someone can turn her facts into a great story. Kind of like *Newsweek,* you know, where they have researchers to do the legwork and writers to put the words together."

Laurie smiled back at him. "I'll try," she said, "but I can't do it here—too much confusion." She gestured at the swirl of people eddying through the room. "I'll take it home and see if I get inspired."

"Terrific," he said. "But you better make a copy so you can leave that one here. I never like to have only one copy of anything important."

"Sure," Laurie said. As she walked down the

long corridor to the copy room, she thought, It would be handy to have a copier in the *Pryer* office, but at least this way I can get some exercise.

Millie Banks turned as Laurie came in. "Hi, Laurie," she said almost under her breath. Her cheeks flamed with color.

Laurie realized that the last time she'd seen Millie was when Chuck was talking to her in the school office. Thinking about Chuck left her oddly unmoved for the first time. He was probably just using Millie to show me he didn't care about me anymore, she thought dispassionately. It would be his style.

She smiled at Millie. "Seems like I see you every time I have to copy stuff for the *Pryer,*" she said cheerfully, punching the "print" button on the copy machine. "What are you copying today?"

"Vocabulary lists for Spanish One," Millie replied. "It's not very exciting, especially because I take French."

Laurie looked at the other girl, surprised that she'd made an attempt at a joke. As she gathered up her copies from the bin, she suddenly felt sorry for Millie. She never seemed to be involved in any after-school activities, and she didn't seem to have a lot of friends. Laurie couldn't remember ever seeing Millie just hanging out with a group. On an impulse she said, "Why don't you come and work on the *Pryer*? It's really fun."

Millie looked up from the papers she was stacking. "I can't," she said quietly. "I don't have time to do anything like that."

"Oh." Laurie wasn't sure how to respond, but at last she said, "Well, if you ever do, come on down to the office. See you later."

Walking back, Laurie thought, It must be hard to work after school every day and then work weekend evenings at the supermarket. Between working and studying, Millie doesn't get much time to have fun.

When she got back to the *Pryer* office, Laurie realized that the room had emptied almost completely. Everyone must be out taking photos or gathering information or whatever, she thought. Besides Mark, only Sean was there, typing madly and muttering at the computer as usual.

Mark greeted her with a smile. "I've just been looking at this profile Richard turned in about Mr. Drake, the new PE teacher. Did you know he was a swim champion in high school—went to the state finals a couple of times—and then he was in the navy SEALs? I'd love to talk to him sometime, I've always wanted to learn to scuba dive."

Laurie pretended to shudder. "Not me," she said. "I like to stay on the surface, where I can see what's going on."

"Oh, but it must be so cool to get down there with the fish," Mark said. "I was reading about some guy who made his own underwater camera with a gyroscope or something to balance it. Makes you think it's worth studying physics after all." He grinned, and Laurie smiled back at him.

Gathering up her books and preparing to leave, Laurie said, "I'll see you tomorrow."

"Not tomorrow," Mark told her. "Office is closed. I've got to go for a scholarship interview, and Hilary has a dentist appointment. But we'll all be here on Friday."

"Okay," Laurie said. "See you then."

CHAPTER 7

AFTER SCHOOL ON THURSDAY, LAURIE went to the library. It had not been a good day. Mr. Bilakian had been very sarcastic in chemistry class when Laurie couldn't get her experiment to work properly. And then, while Amy went for pizza with Richard, Laurie sat with a couple of other girls at lunch. When Roberta Miller asked if Laurie wanted a ride to the football game Friday night, there was an awkward silence before Laurie replied that she wasn't planning to go.

Now Laurie felt a pang of loneliness. She didn't exactly begrudge Amy her blossoming romance with Richard, but it wasn't going to be a fun year if her best friend was busy all the time with a boyfriend.

Oh, well, Laurie thought, I might as well get good grades this year if nothing else. She opened her history book and began going over the material they'd covered in class so far. The test was still a couple of weeks away, but Mr. Gordon had made a big point of saying how important the test was, and Laurie wanted to do well on it.

The library was nearly empty this afternoon, and Laurie sat reading and making notes. She frowned and rubbed her eyes—the words seemed to be breaking apart on the page and she couldn't get them back in focus. Then the dull roaring that she'd come to dread began, and Laurie's stomach knotted. She sat and waited for the inevitable sound.

"Oh, please, somebody help me."

The voice had an urgent quality, the desperation sounding even stronger than before. Laurie bent over her book once again, but she couldn't block out the pathetic pleas.

"Help me, please help me."

Standing up quickly, Laurie cast a frantic glance around her. The library tables were empty except for a studious-looking ninth-grade girl working on math problems with a pocket calculator. But could a child be hidden somewhere behind the shelves?

Resisting the urge to look under the tables—she could see there was nothing there anyway—Laurie hurried toward the rows of shelves. No one was in the first aisle and she walked rapidly along, her eyes searching between each set of shelves, hoping to see a small frightened form. But even as she searched she knew there was no child in the library.

Almost running, Laurie returned to her table. She stuffed her books into her bag and left the library. Outside the main door of the school, Laurie stood waiting hopelessly on the steps. As she knew it would, the sad little voice came again.

"Please help me."

It was pulling at her, drawing her down the steps and along the sidewalk. Laurie looked back once. Should she turn around and go home, ignoring the voice? But she couldn't make herself do it. The pitiful cries led her away from the school, and she was compelled to follow.

Almost in a trance, Laurie let the voice lead her. She felt like a puppet being controlled by something outside her own mind. Leaves had begun to fall from the trees and her feet made scuffling sounds, but she hardly heard them. She crossed several streets without pausing, not even glancing to check for oncoming cars. The sky, overcast all day, grew darker as autumn's early twilight approached.

Laurie crossed another street and continued like a sleepwalker to the middle of the block. And there she stopped. She looked up and down the sidewalk. The street seemed completely deserted, no cars moving, no people raking leaves, no children playing.

She was standing outside a tall iron fence, rusty with age and neglect. Behind the fence was a large dark house, partly hidden by ancient evergreen trees whose branches drooped protectively in front of it. The windows were covered with curtains or shades, and no light glimmered from behind them.

The voice was no longer calling to Laurie. But why had she felt she must stop here? Was the voice coming from inside this old house?

A scrawny gray cat wriggled through the iron fence near Laurie's feet. It stood looking warily at her. Laurie sank down on her heels and held out her hand. "Here, kitty."

As the cat stretched out its neck to give a cautious sniff, Laurie looked up at the house again. At a window on the first floor, the curtain twitched back slightly at one side. Through the dirty glass Laurie could dimly see a face, staring out at her.

A trickle of fear ran down her spine and she stood up abruptly. The little cat raced away down the sidewalk. Then Laurie saw the front door of the house slowly begin to open.

Her heart pounding in her chest, Laurie turned and walked quickly away. She looked back once at the house, but the tall evergreens concealed it from her view.

At the corner, Laurie stopped, still trembling. She looked around, feeling as if she'd just awakened from a trance, and wondered where she was. Then she recognized the houses on the next block. She wasn't far from where Amy lived—a neighborhood in the opposite direction from school and her own home.

She began moving again, almost breaking into a run as she thought of the safe haven she'd find at Amy's house. But in a moment she stopped. There was no way she could deal with normal conversation and normal people right now. Turning the other way, she trudged down three blocks to the main road and the bus stop.

Slumped on the bench waiting for the bus to come, Laurie thought back on what had happened. The whole episode hardly seemed real, now that she was here with other people watching the traffic go by. But the memory of that voice pulling her she didn't know where made her shudder again in remembered fear.

All the next day Laurie thought about the voice and where it had taken her. After school she and Amy worked at the *Pryer* office, in a hubbub of confused activity and laughter. As they left, Amy said, "Are you doing anything tonight?" When Laurie shook her head, Amy continued, "Well, why don't you come over? I have to baby-sit, so I'm stuck at home, but we can rent a video for the brats and one for us to watch after they go to bed."

"Sure, sounds great," Laurie told her. She thought, It may be selfish, but I'm glad Amy has to baby-sit and can't go out with Richard or something. I don't want to sit home by myself tonight.

"Oh, good, now I'll have a sane person to talk to—sometimes my brothers make me absolutely crazy. Hey, Laurie, listen, why don't you sleep over? Then we'll have lots of time to talk."

"Great, see you later."

Her dad wasn't home when Laurie let herself into the house. She fed Casey and then gathered up her overnight stuff. I'd better leave a note for Dad, she thought. Scribbling *I'm at Amy's overnight, see you tomorrow,* she hung the note on the door of the refrigerator where her dad was sure to find it. She was almost ready to leave when the phone rang.

"Hi, Laurie, it's Mom. How are you?"

"Oh, hi, Mom, I'm fine."

"Honey, I'm sorry I didn't call you back until now. I was out of town for a few days." Laurie listened as her mother explained that she'd borrowed a friend's weekend house in the mountains to get away and have some time to think. "I really want to see you, Laurie, but I'm afraid this weekend isn't going to work out. There's a crafts fair in Millbrook and my friend Andrea and I have made plans to go. It's all day tomorrow and Sunday. So I wouldn't really have much time to spend with you."

She paused, and Laurie said quickly, "That's okay, Mom, no problem."

After a moment her mother said, "Well, I do want to see you. What about next weekend? Would you like to come on Saturday and stay the night?"

"Sure," Laurie said, "that sounds fine."

There was a brief silence, and then her mom said, "All right. Should I pick you up or—"

"No," Laurie broke in, "I'll just take the bus. I'll probably come around ten o'clock."

When they'd hung up, Laurie thought, Why is it so hard to talk to Mom? She sounded like I was a total stranger and she didn't know what to say to me. I wish I lived in a normal family. I hate feeling like I have to be careful what I say all the time to Mom and Dad, and knowing that they're being so careful what they say to me.

Laurie bent to scratch Casey's head. "Bye, Casey, be good and I'll be home tomorrow." As she closed the door behind her and started down the hill toward the bus stop, she thought it was lucky that Granville had a decent bus service or she'd never be able to go anywhere. And at least it meant that Mom wouldn't have to come and pick her up at the house next Saturday and maybe run into Dad. Laurie shuddered. That was all she needed—to watch the two of them trying to be polite to each other while she tried to pretend she was invisible.

Amy yanked open her front door as Laurie was climbing the last step up to the porch. "Saw you coming," Amy explained. "And boy, am I glad you're here. One more minute alone with this crowd and I think I might seriously consider homicide as a good alternative to sisterly love." She turned and yelled, "Billy, leave that stuff alone, I told you Mom said it's for dinner, not snacks!"

Life at the Robertses' house usually seemed to Laurie like standing in the middle of a whirlwind. Amy's ten-year-old brother Tim and eight-year-old brother Billy always had gangs of friends around, running in and out of the house for cookies or baseball mitts or something else they urgently needed. Amy's mom worked part-time in an office at the junior college a few miles away, and she also seemed to be on the board of every organization in town. The phone rang constantly and it was almost impossible to keep track of who was doing what and when. It was all so different from Laurie's quiet house.

By eight o'clock Amy and Laurie felt as if they'd fed spaghetti to at least twenty ravenous kids, but finally most of the boys' friends went home and Tim and Billy sat down in the family room to watch a video about aliens from outer space. Laurie and Amy sank onto the living-room couch. Amy heaved an exaggerated sigh. "Peace at last!"

Laurie laughed. "Yeah, there sure were a lot of them. I don't know how you keep their names straight. I felt like I'd never seen some of those kids before and I come over here a lot."

"Oh, there's a million kids in this neighborhood—enough to start a whole school, I think. It's great for my brothers, and for baby-sitting jobs, too." Amy grinned. "But actually you never did see two of those kids who were here before. They just moved into a house on Poplar Street—I think it's about two blocks away—and of course they joined Tim and Billy's bunch of friends right away."

Poplar Street—was that the street the voice had led her to the day before yesterday? Laurie wondered. She said slowly, "Is Poplar Street where that weird house is—the one with the tall iron fence around it?"

Amy looked at Laurie and rolled her eyes. "Oh, yeah, you mean the one with all the big evergreen trees in front of it?" Laurie nodded and Amy went on, "Weird isn't even the word for it. Those people are actually kind of scary. I mean, we don't even know them or know their name or anything, but when Tim was selling peanuts last spring, you know, to raise money for his team's baseball uniforms, he went to every house in this entire neighborhood. Anyway—" Amy paused for breath and a sip of her soda. "So he went to that house and knocked on the door, and this man came and opened the door about two inches, and before Tim could even say anything, the guy told him to get off his property and never come back. He was kind of snarling, Tim said, not loud but really mean sounding. Tim was scared and he said he'd never go back there again for anything."

Laurie stared at her friend. "So you don't know who lives there, I mean, besides the guy Tim saw?"

Amy shook her head. "No, no one ever sees anybody at that house as far as I know, and personally I don't care if I ever meet them, the guy was so nasty to Tim." She looked curiously at Laurie. "What were you doing there, anyway?"

Laurie shrugged. "Oh, I had to go someplace and I was walking back to the bus when I passed the house. I thought it looked kind of spooky."

"Yeah, a haunted house right in my neighborhood." Amy laughed. "Wouldn't it be great if a movie company decided to use it for one of those horror movies?"

Relieved that Amy seemed to have moved on to another subject, Laurie wished once again that she could tell Amy everything—about the voice she kept hearing, and about why she'd been standing in front of the strange old house. But Amy was such a practical, down-to-earth person, she'd think Laurie was weird. And Laurie just couldn't take that risk.

But later that evening, as the two girls sat watching TV, Laurie wondered who really lived in that dark, shuttered house.

CHAPTER 8

AFTER LAURIE WENT HOME FROM AMY'S on Saturday, it seemed that the rest of the weekend dragged along interminably. The only halfway interesting thing she did was to figure out a way to jazz up Hilary's article for the *Pryer* on homelessness. But that didn't take up much of her time, and by Monday morning Laurie couldn't wait to get to school.

In history class she couldn't help noticing that Chuck was carefully and obviously ignoring her. When the buzzer rang, Chuck was one of the first out of the room, and as Laurie walked out, continuing a friendly argument with Richard about Benjamin Franklin, Chuck glanced at her quickly. Then he turned to Meryl, who had been waiting for him, and flung his arm around her shoulders.

Ignoring him in her turn, Laurie walked toward her locker. What a jerk, she thought. I wonder if he's found someone else to copy the history homework from—it wouldn't be worth copying Meryl's. In spite of herself, she smiled. First prize for cattiness, Laurie.

Chemistry lab was difficult and complicated, and Laurie stayed there through most of lunch period trying to complete the experiment and take decent notes. Finished at last, she raced to the cafeteria to grab a sandwich, and then had to hurry back to her locker for her math stuff. She took a quick look to make sure she had everything—but where was her red pen? Ms. Simons was a fanatic on the subject; everyone had to have a red pen to make corrections on the homework, and anyone who didn't have one got marked down a grade no matter what.

She was pawing through her bag, muttering, "I know I had it this morning, but where—" when she heard someone behind her.

"What's the matter, Laurie?" It was Millie Banks.

Laurie brushed her hair out of her eyes. "Oh, hi, Millie. Nothing's wrong, except I can't find my stupid red pen that I need for math class and if I don't have it Ms. Simons will probably have me drawn and quartered."

"You can borrow mine," the other girl said shyly. She reached into her purse and pulled out a red felt-tip pen.

"Really? You don't need it?" Laurie asked. When Millie shook her head, Laurie said, "Hey, thanks—you just saved my life. I'll give it back to you after school, okay?"

As she rushed off (Ms. Simons's room was in

the other wing of the building, of course) Laurie thought, It's lucky that Millie came along when she did. She's pretty nice, even though she's so shy, and she's definitely the organized type.

When she got to the *Pryer* office after school, Laurie realized that she'd been looking forward to it all day. She listened as Mark explained once again to everyone that he wanted the *Pryer*'s first issue to really make a splash. "So we need an important article, something that will make everyone think the *Pryer* has got its act totally together."

Laurie waited until the first burst of activity was over, and then said to Mark, "I need to talk to you about the homeless article." The two of them sat down and she pulled out the first draft Hilary had written. "I thought about this a lot over the weekend, and it seems to me the problem is this is all too dry. It needs something to make it come alive. So what if we had some interviews with a few homeless people? Maybe we could talk to three or four people in depth, you know, to find out what it's really like every day to be homeless, what they hate about it, how they manage if they have kids and all, what they are hoping for."

Before she'd finished speaking, Mark's brown eyes shone with enthusiasm. "You're right, it's a great idea! And it's the perfect concept for the big article. We'll figure out a way to relate all the other stuff to it and tie the whole issue together around this theme. I love it!" In a burst of exuberance, Mark leaned over and hugged Laurie hard. "Listen, Laurie, start writing down all your ideas about this so we can go over them later and divide them up for different people to handle, okay?"

A couple of hours later Laurie was sitting in Pop's Pizza with Mark. Energy seemed to flow through his whole body as he made notes on a piece of paper, gulped soda from the can in front of him, and impatiently pushed away the lock of hair that kept falling into his eyes. His excitement was contagious, and Laurie found herself swept up in his plans for approaching the subject from different angles. Soon she was giggling helplessly at a particularly outrageous idea that somehow involved getting the mayor to write a research paper and setting up a debate between the police chief and the minister of the Lutheran church.

"But that's only the first step," she sputtered through her laughter. "The next thing will be that we all go to Washington and make a speech in the Senate."

Mark grinned. "Hey, who knows? Stranger things have happened. But seriously, Laurie . . ." He reached across the table and took her hand in his. "This is going to be a great issue, and it's so much more important and exciting than just reporting on school stuff like football and whether ninth graders can leave campus for lunch." He glanced up at the clock on the wall. "Hey, it's late, we'd better get out of here."

Outside, Mark seemed to assume that he would drive Laurie home in his battered old Ford. In between getting directions to her house, he asked lots of questions, and Laurie was amazed at how easy he was to talk to. When he pulled up in front of her house, she turned to him. "Thanks a lot, Mark, for the pizza and the ride." And for the great afternoon, she added silently.

"Hey, don't thank me." Mark grinned at her. "I'm just glad you decided to join the *Pryer* this year."

Laurie smiled back. "Me, too."

As she got out of the car he began to half sing, half chant, "Yes, indeedy, don't you love smart women."

Laurie walked into the house, happier than she'd been in a long time.

That night in the kitchen Laurie's father asked, "Did you talk to your mother about a weekend visit?"

Happy that she'd done it before he'd asked, Laurie replied, "Oh, yeah, I guess I forgot to tell you. I'm going to her place on Saturday, and I'll spend the night."

"Oh, good." He looked relieved. "I'm sure you two will have a lot of catching up to do." After a pause he went on, "Listen, Laurie, I know this whole thing, with your mom and me and the divorce, has been hard on you. It's been hard on all of us, and I wish it hadn't had to happen. But it did, and there's no use pretending."

He stopped again and Laurie gazed at him seriously. Where was all this leading? she wondered.

Her dad took a deep breath. "Well, anyway, I don't know what's going on with you and your mom, and that's between you and her, but I just wanted to say, try not to give her a rough time. She loves you a lot, Laurie."

Surprised, Laurie said quickly, "I know, Dad." As she walked upstairs Laurie thought, I don't understand what makes him think I would give Mom a rough time. Then she shrugged. Parents—who could figure them out?

Every afternoon that week Laurie went to the *Pryer* office, sometimes doing some of the thousands of odd jobs that were always waiting, other times proofreading for Sean. She loved being there—she felt at home, with Amy and Richard, now an established item, available to talk and joke with and plenty of work that was really fun in disguise. In the constant activity, she didn't get to say much more than hello to Mark, and so she was surprised on Thursday when he followed her into the hall as she was leaving and asked her out for the next night.

She wasn't even sure what she'd answered, except that Mark had understood she meant yes.

By seven o'clock on Friday Laurie had changed her clothes three times, finally deciding on her new forest-green sweater and jeans—she didn't think Mark was the dressy type. She checked her reflection in the mirror, running a comb one more time through her mane of dark hair and noticing happily that her cheeks had a pink glow of excitement.

When Mark arrived, Laurie opened the door quickly. "Come on," she told him, "I have to introduce you to my dad." This seemed to be one of those awkward rituals that every parent insisted on, and Laurie felt a bit embarrassed to be subjecting Mark to it. But he didn't seem to mind at all. He shook Mr. Carr's hand and answered his questions with equanimity—yes, they were going to a movie and then maybe for something to eat; no, they wouldn't be too late—while Laurie shifted impatiently from one foot to the other.

After the movie, which Laurie and Mark agreed was terrible in spite of glowing reviews, they went to the diner. There they got involved in a discussion about saving the rain forests and whose responsibility they were. Back in Mark's little Ford, they were still talking about carbon dioxide when Laurie realized that Mark wasn't driving toward her house. In a few minutes he pulled into the bumpy dirt parking lot next to the lake just outside of town.

Several other cars were scattered around the edges of the parking lot. It was the place where high-school couples went after a date, but Laurie had never been there before.

Mark looked at Laurie almost shyly. "Too cold to go for a walk?"

Not trusting herself to speak, Laurie shook her head, and soon the two of them were walking single file on a narrow path along the water's edge. When they reached a large rock that overhung the shoreline, Mark stopped. "Let's sit down and look at the moon."

Without waiting for her answer, he climbed up on the rock and turned to take her hand and pull her up. When she sat down beside him, she felt his arm go around her shoulders.

The lake was beautiful, with the moon making a path of light across the shallow ripples. The only sound was the rustle of dry leaves, stirred by the same breeze that ruffled the water.

"Please, somebody help me!"

Laurie stiffened in shock and dismay. She'd almost forgotten about the voice, pushed it out of her mind. and now it was back, faint but clear and sadder than ever. She stared unseeingly straight ahead, her jaws clenched rigidly and her hands grasping one another hard in her lap.

"Laurie, what's wrong?"

Laurie couldn't answer. Despairingly she thought, Maybe if I concentrate, it will just go away. But she knew it wouldn't.

Mark's arm tightened around her shoulders, but her whole body felt stiff and unyielding. As if she were watching herself from far away, she wondered, Is the voice as real as Mark, or is it more real? She heard his concern as he asked gently, "What is it, Laurie?"

Suddenly she blurted out, "It's a voice—a little kid calling for help, and I keep hearing it."

Please don't laugh, she begged him silently. Even if you think I'm nuts, don't laugh.

But Mark didn't laugh. He looked at her seriously for a moment. "What is the voice saying?"

And then the whole story came tumbling out, though she tried to stop herself. She told Mark how she'd first heard the voice in the middle of the night a couple of weeks earlier, calling so pitifully for help, and how since then she'd heard it several more times. "And I know it sounds completely weird, but even though I can't understand how it can be real, I somehow know that it is."

She fell silent and sat looking down at her hands. How could she have been so stupid as to tell Mark about the voice? He must think she was one of those crazy people you read about in books, like the guys whose voices tell them to kill people or run naked through the streets.

At last Mark said, "Wow, Laurie, that's pretty amazing. And it just started a couple of weeks ago out of the blue?"

Laurie turned her head to look at him—he certainly wasn't laughing or making fun of her. Hesitantly she replied, "Well, yes, it just started, and I have no idea why. But—well, when I was younger, about three years ago, I heard some other voices—or at least I thought I did."

"Really?" Mark shifted around to sit cross-legged facing Laurie. He took both of her hands in his. "Will you tell me about them?"

Laurie searched his face. His dark eyes held only sympathetic interest. But she'd already said more than she had wanted to; every detail she added would only make it worse. Don't be an idiot, she told herself, it can't get much worse. She felt his strong hands holding hers. I have to trust someone, she thought.

"I guess so." Laurie looked out across the lake and took a deep breath. "Once I woke up during the night because I heard a kid that sounded like he was drowning. I thought it was this little boy I used to baby-sit for. I was so scared I got up and went to the park where I used to take him and looked to see if he was in the stream." She made a sarcastic noise. "But of course he wasn't, and when I called his mom the next day, he was home in bed with a cold."

She stopped again. After a moment Mark said, "Who else did you hear?"

Staring down at Mark's hands covering her own, Laurie said softly, "My mom. See, my parents split up a few years ago and my mom lives in Bridgeton now. She's had a lot of problems—mental problems, I guess you'd call them. And one day when I was home by myself, I heard her voice saying a lot of stuff. It made me think she was going to kill herself. I tried to call her, but no one answered. So then I got really terrified and I took the bus over to where she lives—and she was there and everything was fine." Laurie stopped again, feeling as though she might be about to cry. She swallowed hard and went on, "So I guess the voices aren't real, even though I think they are when I hear them. And it frightens me." Laurie was almost whispering now. "It makes me think I must be going crazy, like my mom."

It was the first time she'd said it out loud. Laurie slowly raised her eyes to Mark's face, terrified of what she might see there. He smiled at her troubled expression and squeezed her hands reassuringly.

"Well, one thing I know for sure, you're definitely not crazy," he said seriously. "And there's got to be some logical explanation for the voices you hear. You just have to figure out what it is."

Laurie stared at him. "You mean you think the voices I hear are real?"

Mark shrugged. "I don't know, but I think it's possible. I mean, plenty of people all through history have believed that people could talk to each other with their minds. You know, paranormal communication and all that."

"But it doesn't make any sense!" Laurie told him despairingly.

"Somehow it has to, Laurie. I've got this book at home about paranormal communication—some of it's kind of weird but maybe there's something that will give us some clues." He grinned. "Don't worry, we're going to figure this out."

He pulled her close. As her arms went around him Laurie whispered, "Thanks, Mark—thanks a lot."

CHAPTER 9

STANDING OUTSIDE THE DOOR OF HER mother's apartment the next morning, Laurie was determined to make the weekend go well. A warm glow still enveloped her when she thought of Mark. It was amazing, and wonderful, that he hadn't laughed at her or thought she was crazy or even inventing the whole thing. She was so lucky to have met him!

Just make an effort to be nice, she told herself. You can talk to her—she's your mother, after all.

"Hi, honey," her mother said, opening the door. "I just got up—must have overslept. Come on in."

Laurie walked into the small living room, "Hey, you got some new pillows for the couch," she said. "They're great. I love the colors!"

Her mom smiled. "Yes, I saw them at the crafts fair last weekend and fell in love with them. The woman who makes them has a weaving studio up in the country somewhere and I think I'm going to go up and see it sometime. I've been thinking about trying some fabric design."

Laurie nodded. While her mother went into the kitchen to start the coffee Laurie looked around the apartment. She hadn't been here for a while, and it looked a lot more put together than it had last time she'd visited. Her mother had a wonderful feel for fabric and colors—she should have been an interior decorator, Laurie thought, she'd be great at it.

When she sat down at the tiny kitchen table, her mother asked, "How's school this year?"

"Oh, it's okay. You know, some hard classes and some easy ones," Laurie answered. "And I've started working on the *Pryer*—the school newspaper."

"That's nice." Laurie's mom smiled quickly. "I worked on the newspaper when I was in high school."

Buttering a piece of toast, Laurie said, "I didn't know that. That's neat. Well, anyway, it's fun, and Mark asked me to fix up Hilary's article, and now it's turning into the main focus of the whole issue. And Sean said—"

Laurie glanced across at her mom. She looked kind of sad, almost as if she might cry. What had Laurie said wrong?

Nervously Laurie asked, "Mom? What's the matter?" For a long moment she thought her mother hadn't heard her. Then she saw her mom's eyes blink and focus on her again.

"Nothing, honey. It's just a little hard to keep

up with all your new friends." She ran her hands through her short dark hair and gave Laurie a tentative smile. "Well, Laurie, what do you want to do today?"

Laurie shrugged uncomfortably. "I don't care—whatever you want."

"Well, there's an art exhibit I'd like to see at the gallery in the mall." Anna Carr looked questioningly at her daughter. Laurie thought it was almost as if she were asking for permission. "And then, as long as we're there, I thought I'd like to look for a raincoat. My old one is getting pretty shabby."

"Okay with me," Laurie said. At least it might be easier to find stuff to talk about at the mall. More enthusiastically she added, "And I've been wanting to go to Sneaker Pete's anyway and look for some shoes, so that will work out fine."

While her mom went to shower and dress, Laurie wandered around the apartment. She picked up a brochure that was lying on the desk; it was from the local branch of the state university and one page had the corner turned down. Curious, Laurie opened it and saw that a course in interior design had been circled in pen. Gosh, maybe Mom's planning to go back to school, she thought. She wondered if she should say anything about it.

Out of her bathrobe and showered and dressed, Mrs. Carr looked totally elegant. Not for the first time Laurie wished she knew how to make an old shirt, a pair of pants, and a blazer jacket turn into an up-to-date fashionable outfit. She recognized the jacket—she'd been with her mom four years ago when she'd bought it—but somehow the effect was different. Maybe it's the belt, Laurie told herself, like in all those magazine articles about accessories that magically renew your whole wardrobe. She grinned to herself as they walked out the door.

Though looking at paintings at an art gallery wasn't Laurie's idea of the best way to spend a Saturday, when they got there she had to admit that her mom had some interesting observations on the paintings and what they might mean. At first all Laurie could see was swirls of glowing colors, but after a while she began to recognize the relationships among the shapes.

In the first shop they went to, Laurie waited while her mother tried on at least a hundred raincoats, eventually rejecting all of them. One was too short, one too full, another was a horrible color, still another had ugly sleeves. In the next store Laurie liked a midnight-blue one that was cut in a military style, but after trying it on several times, her mom still wasn't sure about it. "I just don't know," she said, talking to herself as well as to Laurie. "It does look quite nice, but it's awfully expensive and I'm not sure it's as practical as some others would be. Oh, honey, I'm sorry I'm taking so long, but . . ."

If she dithers on about this much longer, Laurie thought, I'm going to scream. Aloud she said, "Mom, let's take a break and go look at sneakers. Then we can come back here if you want to look at any of these again."

Her mother seemed relieved at this suggestion. How am I going to keep things going until tomorrow? Laurie thought. At some moments, like in the art gallery, her mom seemed totally normal and together. But choosing a raincoat seemed to make her fall apart. And Laurie felt as if every time she opened her mouth, she managed to say the wrong thing.

Sneaker Pete's was on the lower level of the mall, along with a bookstore, a sports-equipment shop, and several open-air food bars of various kinds. As she walked in, Laurie spotted the back of a familiar head of blond flyaway hair. "Amy! What are you doing here?"

Amy looked up quickly from the shoelaces she was tying. "Hi, Laurie! Gosh, I'm glad to see you. I was supposed to come shopping with my mom today, but at the last minute she had some emergency committee meeting she had to go to, so I came by myself, and it's so *boring* to shop all by yourself. No wonder I never do it if I can help it. Why didn't you tell me you were coming over here today? We could have come together."

By this time Anna Carr was standing next to Laurie. "Mom, this is my friend Amy Roberts," Laurie told her.

Amy was now standing up, bouncing on her toes to test the shoes. "Oh, hi," she said, "it's really nice to meet you, Mrs. Carr." She stared intently into the mirror propped against the wall, then glanced at Laurie and her mother. "What do you think of these sneakers? Are they too weird? They're super comfortable, but will I feel like a duck wearing them?"

Laurie laughed, but her mother looked at Amy's feet, considering the sneakers carefully. "Well, the red stripe along the sides does make quite an aggressive statement, doesn't it?"

"Do you think that's the problem?" Amy asked eagerly. "Maybe you're right. They come in another style, where the stripe is just white like the rest of the shoe, so it blends in more." She picked up a sneaker from the display table to show them.

The salesclerk appeared, and while Amy asked to see the other shoes Laurie told him what she was looking for. When he returned, he had bad news. "I'm sorry, miss, we're out of your size in that sneaker," he told Laurie. "It's a very popular shoe." Turning to Amy, he said, "And we don't have the white on white in your size either. That's last year's model and there aren't many left."

Sighing, Laurie said, "That's always the way—the shoes I want are *never* available in my size."

It was after three o'clock, and as they emerged from the store Laurie realized that she was starving. As if she'd read her mind, her mother said, "I think I'd like to sit down and have something to eat. Let's go over there—"

She gestured across the open court. "There's a place that has imported coffees and teas and wonderful pastries."

It was hard to choose among the tempting array of flaky croissants and sticky buns, but eventually they were settled at a tiny table next to the indoor fountain. Laurie had decided to try mint tea, and it was deliciously light and delicate. She sipped it, listening to Amy chatter to her mom about her family.

"And so sometimes it gets kind of boring being the oldest and bossing my brothers around." Amy laughed. "So I'm happy to escape now and then. Did Laurie tell you we're both working on the *Pryer* and trying to get the first issue ready to be printed at last?"

"Well, she did mention something about it." Anna Carr glanced fondly at Laurie. "I'm awfully pleased—you can learn a lot working on a school newspaper. What exactly are the two of you doing?"

"Lots of odd jobs." Laurie laughed. "Proofreading, photocopying, running around for this or that. It's mostly the seniors who have the important jobs, or the people who worked on the *Pryer* last year."

"Yeah, so maybe next year Laurie and I will be running the whole thing," Amy chimed in. "But Laurie had this great idea of doing interviews with some homeless people—the theme of our first issue is going to be the homeless problem—and so she's busy helping everyone set up the interviews."

"My goodness." Laurie's mother looked impressed. "It sounds like a pretty interesting paper. Will you bring me a copy when it comes out?"

"Sure," Laurie told her, "although who knows when that will be." She poured more mint tea, admiring the pale green tint against the white cup. "Wouldn't these be good colors for a summer dress?"

Her mother peered into the cup. "Yes, they're very restful. It would be a marvelous color scheme for a bedroom, with maybe a bedspread in graduated shades of green."

"That can be your first project for your fabric designs," Laurie told her.

"Oh, are you a designer?" Amy asked.

"No, no," Laurie's mother began, but Laurie said quickly, "You said you were going to talk to that weaving lady and try doing it." Turning to Amy, she added, "Mom's got great taste—you should see the way she's fixed up her apartment." Soon they were all involved in a discussion of favorite colors and patterns, and which kinds of designs worked best in different kinds of rooms.

When Laurie's mother left to go and find a ladies' room, Amy said, "Gosh, Laurie, your mom is so nice. And she's really pretty. I'm glad I finally got to meet her. You guys must have a lot of fun together."

"Yeah, we do," Laurie answered automatically. Amy's words had surprised her, and she was struggling to make sense of them. Amy was right, this afternoon had been fun. Obviously Mom and Amy had enjoyed talking to each other. Of course, Amy didn't know how hard Laurie had been working before at keeping the conversation going with her mom. Amy can talk to anyone, Laurie thought. Then she realized in surprise, I guess Mom can, too—she didn't have any trouble chatting away with Amy. Maybe it's just me she can't talk to.

But that could be because she knows I feel kind of nervous around her, Laurie thought. Mom probably can sense that I'm always worried she'll have another breakdown. Unwillingly Laurie admitted to herself that that might be enough to make anyone act a little bit odd.

As she sipped her tea and waited for her mother to return, Laurie wondered if she could have been exaggerating her mom's problems all this time. Had she been making things worse between them? And had she been keeping her mother shut out of her life for no good reason?

CHAPTER 10

AT THE *PRYER* OFFICE AFTER SCHOOL on Monday, Mark seemed full of energy he could barely contain. At five o'clock he declared that he was finished for the day and practically dragged Laurie out to the parking lot. Before they even reached his car, he had begun talking, his eyes flashing with intensity.

"I've been thinking about your voices all weekend," he told her. "I went to the library downtown to look up a bunch of stuff. I wanted to see if I could find any cases that sounded like yours."

"Cases of what?" Laurie asked.

"Well, ESP, or some other kind of paranormal communication," he replied. "I don't know exactly what. That's why I need to ask you some questions."

He was driving out to the lake again, though the day was overcast and quite chilly. As they walked along the path to the large flat rock they'd sat on before, Laurie was glad she'd worn a heavy sweater.

They sat down facing the gray water, choppy today with small whitecaps, and Mark said, "Okay, we're going to start out with the idea that you are not crazy. Agreed?"

Laurie smiled slightly. "Yes, agreed."

"All right, then, that means the voices you've heard are not figments of your imagination. And, making a logical deduction, that means that they are real in some way." He held up one hand as if to stop Laurie from speaking, though in fact she hadn't intended to say anything. "Now, I know you're going to say that the things you heard people say didn't really happen. So let's say you're right about that. But that doesn't mean much. My theory is that you heard their *thoughts,* even if they didn't actually say the stuff you heard out loud."

He paused for breath, and Laurie stared at him. It was amazing, and somehow very reassuring, that Mark took her voices so seriously. He'd taken up the challenge of finding out what the whole thing meant. Though Laurie wasn't sure that Mark or anyone else could explain the voice she'd been hearing lately, it made her feel good that he was trying.

"Okay, so let's get some answers and see if my theory holds up," he was saying. "First of all, when you heard your mom and you thought she was going to commit suicide, what did she actually say? Do you remember?"

"Oh, yes." Laurie shivered—there was no way she could have forgotten those words that had scared her so. “She was crying, and she said, ‘What’s the use, I can’t stand this any-more. I can’t go on, I’d be better off dead.’”

“Right,” Mark said. “And had something hap-pened right around that time that would have made her feel upset or depressed?”

Laurie thought about his question. “I don’t really know,” she said slowly. “My dad and I had just moved into the house we live in now. She was supposedly going to move there with us, too, only they split up before that happened. Before they decided to get divorced, she’d been going to a shrink, because she was sort of screwed up, I guess. And also she quit her job, or maybe she got fired, I’m not too sure exactly what happened. So she hadn’t been very happy for a while, but I don’t know if anything specific happened to make her get upset that day.”

Mark nodded. “And what kind of day was it—bright and sunny?”

Laurie shook her head. “No, it was one of those really dark, gloomy, overcast days where you keep thinking it’s going to rain any minute.”

“Right.” Jumping to his feet, Mark began pacing back and forth on the flat surface of the rock while Laurie twisted around to look at him. “So doesn’t this make sense? Your mom was upset and feeling totally down, and she was thinking stuff like, Oh, what’s the use. And you were hearing her thoughts. It’s kind of like you were tuning in on another wavelength—not catching actual sound waves like when people talk, but catching her thoughts. But then, when you went over to her place to see if she was okay, she didn't want to get you upset and worried about her, because you were just a kid, so she pretended everything was fine."

"But she's been upset other times," Laurie protested, "and I haven't heard her."

"Well, maybe that time she was just more upset than she'd ever been before and she wasn't trying to stop thinking those thoughts, or maybe for some reason you were more tuned in to her than usual that day. You were more receptive to her thoughts."

"Well, maybe," Laurie said. She wanted to believe Mark's theory was right, but it didn't exactly explain everything.

As if he'd read her mind Mark said, "Okay, then, what about the kid you heard drowning? Who was he exactly?"

"Well, I thought it was Carlos Weber—he lived a couple of houses away from us when Dad and I first moved to the new house. I baby-sat for him a lot before they moved away. He was four years old, and I used to take him to play in the park down the hill from us where there's this stream that flows down and makes a little pond. Carlos really liked splashing around in the water and building dams and stuff. So when I woke up and heard him, and it sounded like he was choking for breath, and it sounded like water splashing, I was sure he was drowning in the pond."

"Okay, so he wasn't really in the pond when you went to look," Mark said. "But where was he?"

Laurie shrugged helplessly. "He was home. When I called the next day, because I couldn't get him out of my mind, his mom said he'd had a cold and a fever, but he was getting better."

Mark stopped his pacing and plopped down next to Laurie. "Hmm, that doesn't sound very helpful." He stared out at the lake. "Maybe he wasn't actually drowning. Maybe he was choking because he couldn't breathe right, because of having a cold."

"Well, maybe—but if that happened, I didn't know about it." Laurie frowned as she thought back to that time. An elusive memory was struggling to the surface. She turned to Mark. "But actually, I think it was a couple of weeks later when I went to baby-sit, Carlos's mother told me not to bother giving him a bath because he was scared of the bathtub and it wasn't worth the hassle."

"That's it!" Mark's face was alive with enthusiasm. "He must have almost drowned in the bathtub, and that's what you heard!"

"But why would he be in the bathtub at almost midnight?" Laurie objected. "He was just a little kid, he would have been asleep in bed."

"Well, maybe he couldn't sleep because of his

cold, so they were giving him a bath," Mark speculated. "Or wait, I know! He had a fever, right? When I was little, I was sick a lot, and my mom always used to put me in a lukewarm bath to bring my fever down. So let's say he was in the bathtub and they stepped out of the room for a minute and he was so sleepy that he slipped down under the water. How about that?"

Laurie smiled at him. "It does make sense," she said happily. "You'd make a great detective, Mark."

"Psychic mysteries our specialty." Mark grinned, then jumped down from the rock. "Come on, let's walk around, I think better on my feet." He took Laurie's hands to help her down, then set off along the edge of the lake.

"Okay, so now we've got explanations for the voices you heard before, right? And both of them were in trouble, or at least they felt like they were in trouble. So now we just have to figure out who this kid is that's calling to you for help now. It's got to be a real kid that's got some kind of problem."

Laurie shook her head. "But it can't be. I don't know any kids who might be in trouble. There aren't any little kids that live near us, and the only kids I know are other people's little brothers, like Amy's, and they're perfectly okay." She stepped over a fallen tree that lay across the path and sighed in frustration. "If your idea is right, then the voices I heard before were people I was close to—my mom and Carlos. But this voice I've been hearing now can't be like that, because there aren't any little kids I'm close to now."

They had reached the parking lot when Mark turned to face her. "Don't give up, Laurie," he said. "I know we're on the right track here, and there's sure to be an explanation. We just haven't thought of it yet."

They got into the car, and Mark began to turn the key in the ignition, then paused. "You know, maybe we should ask Mr. Carelli what he thinks about this whole thing. He knows a lot about all kinds of paranormal stuff. In fact, he's the one who got me interested in it in the first place last year when we were reading Stephen King and Edgar Allan Poe."

Laurie was shaking her head vehemently. "No, please, Mark, I don't want to talk to him or anyone else about it," she said, her words coming out in a rush. "It's too weird, and, well, I just don't want anyone else to know about it."

"Okay," Mark said, starting the car and backing it away from the trees. "It's up to you."

Was Mark disappointed? Laurie didn't know. Later that night, as she got ready for bed, she wondered whether she was going to be sorry she'd told him about her voices. But she knew she wasn't sorry—he'd made her feel he believed her and he didn't think she was crazy. And certainly he thought there was a logical explanation. Now, if only she could come up with it.

I'm glad I told Mark all about it, she thought as she turned out her light and pushed Casey to the side of the bed. I just hope he won't tell anyone else—I couldn't stand it if people started asking me all about my paranormal experiences or something. Snuggling into the pillow, she thought drowsily, It's nice that Mark doesn't think I'm nuts. But what would be really nice would be if I didn't hear the voice ever again.

Sometime later Laurie woke up abruptly. For a moment she was disoriented. She sat up and blinked hard, peering through the darkness. Shadows played across the far wall and made her room look strange and unfamiliar. Her breath came in short gasps, as if she'd been frightened in her sleep. Did I have a nightmare? she wondered. Then a dull certainty came over her. She knew it hadn't been a nightmare. Her heart sank as she heard the now familiar little voice. "Please, somebody help me!"

Who could it be? She strained to listen closely to the sad call, but she already knew she couldn't recognize the voice's owner. She was no closer to knowing who was crying out for help than she'd been the first time she'd heard it.

Tears of frustration welled up in Laurie's eyes. Casey, sensing her distress, licked her wrist in sympathy.

"Oh, please help me!" The voice was fainter than before.

"Why are you doing this?" Laurie whispered into the darkness. Her voice was choked with tears. "Please just leave me alone!"

Laurie sank back in bed and pulled the covers over her head. But she knew it would be a long time before she slept again.

CHAPTER 11

ALL DAY TUESDAY LAURIE WAS TENSE and anxious, sure that any minute she'd hear the child's voice calling to her again. She found herself glancing nervously over her shoulder, as if someone might be following her. The idea that she might hear the voice was constantly in her mind, no matter how hard she tried to push it away. Only when she got to the *Pryer* office after school and was swept up in the usual frenzied activity did the hunted feeling begin to fade.

Laurie glanced up from proofreading a list of sports scores when Amy walked into the office. Her friend looked as if she had a secret she was dying to share.

Amy dropped her books on a table with a bang. "Listen up, everybody!" When she had everyone's attention, she grinned. "Great news! *Finally,* after a lot of begging and pleading from me, my mom and dad said I could have a Halloween party at our house on Saturday.

So—you guys are the first to know, and this is your official invitation."

A chorus of "Great!" and "What time?" and "Hey, let's wear costumes and scare each other" greeted her announcement.

Amy added, "Oh, yeah, everybody has to come in costume. You won't be allowed in the door unless you're dressed up in something weird."

"Some of us already dress weird," Richard told her, turning his baseball cap backward and jamming it down over his eyes.

Amy laughed. "You said it, I didn't," she said. "But I'm not sure it's weird enough. I'll have to get back to you on that."

After a few minutes Mark sat down next to Laurie, still talking about Amy's announcement. "I haven't been to a Halloween party since eighth grade, I think," he said. "Sounds like a fun idea. But I'd like to come up with a truly mind-boggling costume."

Laurie nodded. "Yeah, that's the hard part. Have you got any ideas yet?"

"How about if we go as Clark Kent and Lois Lane?" Seeing Laurie's puzzled look, Mark explained, "You know, Clark Kent is the newspaper reporter who turns into Superman."

"Well, maybe—what does Lois Lane wear?" Laurie asked.

"I don't know," he told her with a laugh. "We'll have to do some serious research."

"Right." Laurie smiled. "But meanwhile—"

She pulled a list of names out of her bag. "I stopped by Mr. Carelli's room today and he gave me this list we asked for—it's the homeless people he thinks would be willing to be interviewed for the article."

"Oh, great!" Mark picked up a pencil, and soon they were matching reporters with people to be interviewed and making a schedule they hoped would work.

It was late when Laurie got home, and she was relieved that her dad was out for the evening at a seminar. She had a lot of homework and she wanted to start getting serious about preparing for the history test on Friday. Mr. Gordon had emphasized again today that this was an important test and it would count for a lot in the midterm grades. She was still studying when her father got home.

"Hi, honey," he said from the doorway of her room. "Still working?"

Laurie brushed the hair away from her face and gave him a tired smile. "Big test coming up on Friday," she told him. "So I'm trying to learn everything there is to know about the events leading up to the Revolutionary War."

"Sounds like a major undertaking," her dad replied. "I won't disturb you. See you in the morning."

The next afternoon at the *Pryer* office, Sean said to Laurie, "Run over to the copy room and make me fifty copies of this, will you?" Laurie took the sheet of paper from his hand. "It's a final call for information from the teachers for the *Pryer*. If they don't get it to me by Friday, it doesn't get in this issue." Sean drew his finger across his neck in a theatrical gesture. "So after you make the copies, put one in each teacher's box, okay?"

Laurie gave him a mock salute. "Aye, aye, sir," she said with a laugh.

She had almost reached the copy room when she saw Jim DeCicca farther down the hall, leaning against the wall and talking to Meryl Worthing. Suddenly Laurie just wasn't in the mood to wave and say hi to them or, worse, to obviously ignore them and feel their calculating eyes on her back. She ducked into the ladies' room that was conveniently between her and the copy room.

Opening the door, she stopped abruptly. For a moment she swayed and put out a hand to steady herself against the wall. A child was weeping as if its heart would break, and Laurie thought, Oh, no, I don't want to hear that pitiful voice again.

But almost immediately she realized that this wasn't her voice—this time a real person was sobbing inconsolably. Laurie pushed through the inner swinging door and saw Millie Banks. She was sitting on the floor near the sinks, her knees drawn up to her chest and her head bent to muffle her tears. Laurie rushed over and knelt down beside her. "Millie, what's wrong?"

The younger girl shook her head, sending her

fine brown hair flying. "Nothing—leave me alone." The words were hard to distinguish.

Laurie put her hand on Millie's shoulder. What could have happened? Had Millie gotten hurt somehow? But Laurie didn't see any blood, and Millie's sobs didn't sound like those of pain. "Millie," she said again, "please don't cry. What's the matter?"

For a long moment Millie didn't move. Then she lifted her tear-blotched face and looked straight at Laurie. Her reddened eyes made Laurie's throat tighten in sympathy. "Oh, Millie, what is it? Can I help?"

Millie shook her head slowly while tears brimmed again in her eyes. "No," she said softly, "no one can help."

"But what's happened?" Laurie insisted. She held Millie's gaze steadily.

At last Millie sighed heavily. "Oh, Laurie, I've been so stupid." Her voice was so low Laurie had to strain to hear her. "I was doing some work for Mr. Gordon—making copies of the test he's going to give on Friday." She glanced at Laurie, who nodded in understanding. "And when they were done, I stacked them up on the table in the copy room, and then I came in here to use the bathroom, and when I went back—" Millie swallowed hard, and her shaking voice steadied a bit. "Chuck was in the copy room and he was standing right by the table where the test copies were, and he made some kind of joke and then he left. And, oh, Laurie—" Millie gave a convulsive sob and wiped at the tears that had begun streaming down her cheeks again. "I just know he took one of the tests, and it's all my fault, and Mr. Gordon will be so mad. I thought maybe I just wouldn't tell him about it, but I can't do that, I'd feel too awful, but I can't tell on Chuck either, that's being a tattletale, and I just don't know what to do!"

Millie put her head down on her knees again and wept. Laurie patted the girl's shaking shoulder and thought about what she had said. She wouldn't be too surprised, she thought, if Chuck had taken a copy of the test. After his attempt to get Laurie to do his history homework for him, this was just more of the same. Still, it was a pretty serious accusation.

"Millie, what makes you think he took one of the tests?"

The younger girl looked at her bleakly. "Well, he looked kind of guilty when I walked back into the copy room. But besides that—" She gulped and then went on, "He's been asking me stuff about my job and who I do copying for and all, and I mean, it's not like a secret or anything, so I told him. And then, a couple of days ago, he was talking to me again and he mentioned Mr. Gordon's test. He made this big joke, like it would be worth a lot to him to see it and if I happened to make an extra copy of the test for him, Santa Claus might come early to my house this year."

Laurie sighed sympathetically. "Oh, boy. And

I bet you didn't say anything about it to anyone."

Millie shook her head. "How could I? It was a joke. And of course I never even considered taking it seriously or *doing* what he suggested."

"Of course you didn't. But, Millie, are you absolutely certain that Chuck took a copy of the test?"

"Well, I'm pretty sure," the younger girl said slowly. "But I didn't actually see him do it." She glanced over at the decrepit wooden chair in the corner of the room, under the paper-towel dispenser. Laurie followed her glance, and for the first time saw the pile of papers stacked precariously on its slanted seat.

"Is that the test?" When Millie nodded, Laurie went on, "Well, how many did you make?"

"A hundred and fifty-four," Millie replied.

"Okay," Laurie said. "Let's count them, and then you'll know if one is missing." Surely Chuck wouldn't have had a chance to make another copy, she thought—the pages would have to be unstapled and run through one at a time and then stapled together again, and he might easily have been caught.

Millie stood up and stared into the mirror. Her swollen eyes and reddened nose gave her a woebegone appearance. Laurie felt a brief flash of impatience. "Come on, Millie, wash your face and blow your nose and then we'll go count these things."

In the copy room Millie laid the stack of tests

on one of the tables. "Give me half and we'll each count our batch," Laurie suggested. Then, catching Millie's doubtful look, she added, "Turn them upside down—then you'll be sure I can't sneak a peek."

The two of them counted the tests twice and totaled the number. "One hundred and fifty-three," Millie said in a despairing tone. "You see, I was right, he did take one."

"Yes, I guess he must have," Laurie agreed.

Millie's eyes filled with tears once more. "Oh, what am I going to do? When Mr. Gordon finds out, he'll be so angry, and I'll probably get fired from this job, and then my mom will be so upset. And when she hears the reason, she'll ground me for life, I just know it. And besides that, Chuck will be so angry, he'll want to kill me."

Laurie felt a spurt of angry indignation. It probably hadn't been very smart of Millie to leave the tests in the copy room while she went to the ladies' room, but she hadn't done anything dishonest or underhanded. It wasn't fair if she got all the blame for what had happened.

Still, Millie was right, she had to tell Mr. Gordon about it. It would be even more unfair to say nothing and let Chuck prepare his answers to the test questions in advance. Not to mention that he would probably share his information with his friends, giving his little group an undeserved advantage over everybody else who took the test.

Millie raised one hand to her mouth. Laurie saw that it was trembling. Impulsively Laurie took both of Millie's hands in her own. "Millie, you're right, you do have to tell Mr. Gordon what happened. But maybe you don't have to tell him it was Chuck. You can just say you went out to the ladies' room, and when you went back, someone was just leaving the copy room but you couldn't tell who it was. Then tell Mr. Gordon you counted the copies and one is missing. He's a pretty nice guy underneath, I think—he won't eat you alive or anything."

"Yes, okay," Millie said slowly. "But, Laurie, would you come with me? I'm so scared to tell him." Her beseeching gaze didn't leave Laurie's face.

"All right," she said. She walked over to the copy machine and set the counter. "Just wait while I do what I came here to do in the first place."

Standing outside Mr. Gordon's office door, Laurie smiled encouragingly at Millie. "Ready?" When the other girl nodded, Laurie knocked, then opened the door.

Mr. Gordon looked surprised to see Laurie. He said to Millie, "Oh, good, put those over there on that shelf, will you, please?" Then he turned to Laurie. "What can I do for you, Miss Carr?"

"Actually it's Millie that wants to talk to you," she told him.

He looked inquiringly at the younger girl.

Squaring her shoulders and taking a deep breath, Millie blurted out, "Mr. Gordon, I think someone took a copy of the test."

Mr. Gordon waited a moment, but Millie didn't go on. Raising his eyebrows, he asked, "How did that happen?"

Millie blushed painfully. "Well, I made a hundred and fifty-four copies like you told me to, and then I left them stacked up in the copy room while I went to the, um, the ladies' room. When I was walking back, someone came out of the copy room, but I couldn't see who it was. And then when I counted the tests, there were only a hundred and fifty-three."

Millie's voice was quavering by the time she reached the end of this speech. She looked as if she might fall down in a faint. Mr. Gordon said kindly, "Sit down, Miss Banks, and don't look so frightened." Looking at Laurie, he went on, "And where do you come into this, Miss Carr?"

"I had to make some copies for the *Pryer,* and I got to the copy room just after this happened," she explained.

Millie said quickly, "She helped me count the tests, but we turned them upside down so Laurie couldn't see what was on them."

"I don't believe that would have made much difference at this point." Mr. Gordon's voice was dry. "If someone has stolen a copy of the test, a new one will have to be made up."

A tear slipped down Millie's cheek and she brushed at it impatiently. "Oh, Mr. Gordon, I'm so sorry," she cried. "I know it was all my fault, I shouldn't have left the tests in there where anyone could come in and see them. I'm really really sorry."

Mr. Gordon said evenly, "It's true, you should not have left temptation in someone's way. It's a sad reality that there are always people who will cheat if they think they can do it without being caught. And you didn't recognize this person who was leaving the copy room?"

Millie shook her head mutely.

"I see," he went on. "That's too bad. However"—he smiled at Millie—"I think you showed great courage in telling me what has happened, and you've no doubt learned something you won't soon forget. I must take some of the blame myself—it's probably not a good idea to ask a student employee to make copies of sensitive items like tests. I'll bring it up at the next faculty meeting."

Mr. Gordon paused, making a steeple of his hands and resting his chin on them while he gazed abstractedly over Millie's head. At last he looked at both girls. "I think it will be best if you don't say anything about this to anyone—and especially not to anyone whom you might suspect of being the culprit. I will deal with this problem in my own way."

As Millie stood up and the two girls moved toward the door, Mr. Gordon said, "Remember, please, don't discuss this matter with anyone."

"We won't," Laurie and Millie said almost in unison.

"Thank you, Mr. Gordon," Millie added. Then they were standing in the hall outside his office. "Thanks a lot, Laurie," she said.

"It's okay," Laurie told her. "See you later." As she walked back to the *Pryer*, Laurie thought, Mr. Gordon looked like he had some really diabolical plan in mind. I wonder what—but whatever it is, I hope it will give Chuck a nasty surprise. What a creep. She smiled to herself. I can't wait for history class on Friday.

CHAPTER 12

WHEN LAURIE CAME OUT OF CHEM LAB on Thursday, Amy was waiting for her. "Are you having lunch with Mark?" she demanded.

When Laurie told her Mark was busy tutoring a ninth grader in math during lunch, Amy said, "Good! I feel like I haven't had a minute to talk to you for ages!"

As they walked through the crisp fall sunshine to the deli, Laurie thought that Amy was right—they hadn't spent much time together the past week. They'd both been so busy, with homework, the *Pryer,* and of course Mark and Richard. Amy was now telling Laurie that Richard was the funniest, nicest, most interesting boy in the entire school, if not the world. "And you know, he plays saxophone in the band, and I'm *so* glad my mom made me keep taking band this year when I wanted to drop it. I mean, it's a drag getting up early for practice three days a week and I'll never be a seriously terrific flute player, so it didn't really seem worth keeping on. But now it's perfect, there's someone to talk to while Mr. Kane is working with the percussionists, which always takes forever, and it's a great excuse to see Richard without being super obvious, you know?"

Laurie smiled at her friend. "I'm glad the two of you got together."

"Me, too!" Amy said fervently. "And can you believe it, he actually likes the brats, or at least he says he does. He walked me home after the *Pryer* yesterday and he ended up spending about an hour goofing around with them. At first I was a little annoyed, but then I kind of got into it myself, and we had a great time. Laurie, anyone who can have fun with my little brothers has got to be practically a saint."

Amy paused for breath and Laurie asked, "How are your plans for the party coming along?"

"Oh, it's going to be great!" Amy launched into a description of the decorations, the food, her costume (she was planning to dress up as a gypsy fortune-teller with a miniature crystal ball around her neck). "And I got this book for kids about Halloween parties, and it tells how to do a haunted-house thing—you know, where you use cold spaghetti for brains and peeled grapes for eyeballs and stuff like that and you make everyone walk through it with a blindfold on. So I think the brats are going to set that up and take everyone through it, and then they'll be happy and they can go out and do their trick-or-treating and get out of our way for the rest of the time."

"Sounds great!" Laurie said. "I've got to get busy and find a costume—Mark wants us to go as Superman and Lois Lane."

"Neat idea," Amy said. "But what did Lois Lane wear?"

"I had to look up some old stuff about the comics and the Superman movies," Laurie told her. "Mostly she just wore regular dresses or suits that you'd wear to an office, only sort of in a forties style, with a tight waist and fairly long skirt, and sometimes she wore a little hat, but I'm not sure I'm going to go that far. But I'm planning to go to that secondhand-clothes shop near where my mom lives to find something that looks right. Oh, and I was telling my mom about it on the phone, and she's going to come with me to look for a dress that will look okay and not be too expensive."

"Fabulous! And if it's forties style, you can do some great makeup, with dark red lipstick and lots of eyebrow pencil."

"Yeah, if only I can figure out what to do with my hair."

"Well, I've got the same problem—no gypsy ever had frizz like this!" Amy laughed. "Maybe we should go look for wigs."

The big American-history test was the next day, and after school Laurie went straight home, refusing Mark's offer of pizza. "I just can't spare any time today, Mark," she told him regretfully. "I've got a lot of math homework and some reading for English, and I've got to finish all my reviewing for the test tomorrow."

"Okay," he said with a mock sigh. "I remember that test from last year. It was pretty hard, but if you do well on it, you're in good shape for the rest of the year because Mr. Gordon will think you're really paying attention to his class."

Studying that night, Laurie remembered Mark's words and resolved to know the material for the test as well as she possibly could. Somewhat to her surprise, she found it interesting, and reading over her notes from Mr. Gordon's class made her see how he tried to relate things that happened over two centuries ago to events in the world right now. But when she closed her books for the last time and started to get ready for bed, she felt tense and keyed up.

As she reached over to turn off her alarm clock on Friday morning, Laurie realized with a wave of relief that she hadn't been awakened by the voice for several nights. The last time she'd heard it was Monday night, after she'd had that long talk with Mark and listened to his ideas about Carlos and her mom. His explanations had made so much sense and Laurie found she had completely accepted them by now.

But it still left the problem of who the recent voice belonged to. As she'd discussed the whole thing with Mark she'd tried really hard to think of who it might be, but she couldn't think of anyone. Could it possibly be that the voice had been trying to communicate with the wrong person? Had the words she'd heard Monday night been one last try at reaching someone who could help, and had the voice somehow understood that she didn't know who it was or how to help? Flinging back the covers, Laurie thought, I sure hope that's true.

In health class that morning, Laurie could hardly pay attention to Ms. Jenkins's monotonous voice droning on about infectious diseases. She kept sneaking superstitious glances at the list she'd made of important names, dates, and events in the years before the American Revolution. And of course, she couldn't help wondering what Mr. Gordon had decided to do about the test. Laurie had kept her promise not to talk about the stolen test, though she had had to bite her tongue to keep from spilling the whole story to Amy.

As the students settled into their seats in Mr. Gordon's room, most of them looked nervous, arranging pens and pencils in front of them and flipping open textbooks for a last quick review. But Chuck zoomed in at the last minute, calling good-bye to someone in the hall (probably Meryl, Laurie thought) and sliding into his seat with a smile just as the buzzer rang.

"Good morning." Mr. Gordon's voice was dry and cool. "As soon as I've taken attendance, we'll get started with the test, because I want all of you to have as much time as possible to finish it. I've decided to try a different kind of test this year, and you lucky juniors have the chance to be the guinea pigs." He paused and looked around the room. Laurie glanced at Chuck, whose expression was puzzled and a little wary. "There are no objective questions on this test. Instead the test consists of six essay questions," Mr. Gordon went on. "You are to answer any three of them. Keep track of the time so you'll do justice to all three of the questions you choose. You may begin as soon as everyone has a test paper."

As he handed a pile of papers to the first person in each row, Laurie looked once again at Chuck. He certainly isn't smiling now, she thought, he looks sick. And it serves him right. I bet he didn't really study the material, just memorized the answers to the objective questions on the original test.

She took a copy of the test and handed the others to Sheri Anderson in back of her. Then with a final glance at Chuck's stricken face, she began to read the questions.

When the period was over, Laurie set down her pen with a sigh. She felt drained, as if she'd run a marathon, but she thought she'd done pretty well. She'd actually come up with a lot of ideas about the questions Mr. Gordon had posed. All her studying had been worth it, she realized with satisfaction.

Chuck was standing in front of Mr. Gordon's

desk, talking rapidly in a low tone. From the expression on his face, Laurie could tell he was using all his charm. She wondered what he was trying to talk Mr. Gordon into. From the set of Mr. Gordon's mouth, she could tell that he wasn't buying whatever Chuck was telling him. Poor Chuck—he must have really done terribly on the test. And he said if his grades went down, his dad would make him quit football. Then the image of Millie's anguished face flashed across Laurie's mind, and she thought, Why should I feel sorry for him? He's just getting what he deserved.

On Saturday morning Laurie got off the bus in Bridgeton and hurried to meet her mother at Secondhand Rose, the shop whose vast stock ran the gamut from last year's evening gowns back to flapper dresses from the twenties. Boy, I sure hope we find something, she thought. I shouldn't have left this till the very last minute. Still, no one can remember what Lois Lane wore, so I'll just tell everyone that whatever I end up with is the right look.

Smiling, Laurie pushed open the shop's door and waved to her mother, who was standing in front of a rack of blouses.

"Look at this, Laurie!" Mom's eyes were sparkling. She held a soft silk shirt in a beautiful coral shade against her chest. "Isn't it gorgeous? And feel the fabric!" The glowing color set off her dark hair and warmed her creamy complexion.

"Oh, Mom, it's fabulous!" Laurie fingered the material. "And it would feel so good to wear." She peered down at the cuff she was holding. "But there's a stain here. Did you see it?"

"Oh, yes, I know," her mother said. "That's probably why it's so cheap. But I can't find anything else wrong with it. I'll just wear it with the sleeves rolled up." She laughed. "I love finding bargains like this, and I never would have come in here if it hadn't been for you." Holding the shirt on its hanger, she gestured with her other hand to a hook outside the dressing room where three or four dresses were hanging. "While I was waiting for you I couldn't resist looking around, and I found a couple of things that might work for Lois Lane."

The topmost dress was obviously what Lois would wear to the office—a dark blue rayon dress with buttons down the front and a middy collar edged in white. Laurie made a face. It might be the right style for the forties, but it looked totally blah.

"I know," her mother said, seeing her expression. "It's not very exciting, but it's the right period, so I thought you ought to see it. This next one may have the same effect on you."

Setting the middy dress aside, Laurie saw a black-and-white-check suit. The skirt was narrow and very long, with a bunch of little kick pleats across the back below knee level. The jacket was even more peculiar. It had tight sleeves and a fitted body that flared out at the waist in a short rounded peplum. Attached to the left lapel was a large bright red fake rose.

Laurie giggled. "Did people really wear these things? I hope they never had to run for a bus."

But the next dress was gorgeous. It was a black evening dress with a beaded top and a floating skirt of gossamer chiffon. Laurie couldn't resist trying it on. The square low-cut neckline flattered her figure and the yards of chiffon skimmed the floor as she twirled on her tiptoes.

Laurie looked at her mom and sighed. "It's so beautiful, and it fits perfectly. But I don't think it's right for Halloween. Lois Lane probably never got dressed up, and I'd be afraid I'd trip and tear the whole thing."

Her mother nodded. "Too bad—you really look lovely in it." She handed Laurie the remaining dress she'd picked out. "Try this one—I have a feeling it may be just what you're looking for."

Zipping up the back of the dress, Laurie stared at herself in the mirror. Mom was right, she thought, it's perfect. I'd never have thought this dark plum color would look good on me. Graceful and elegant, the dress was made of a fine soft jersey that felt great against her skin. The snug-fitting top accentuated Laurie's slim waist and the gored skirt swirled from her hips as she walked.

Opening the dressing-room door, Laurie struck a dramatic pose. "Ta-da!"

Anna Carr clapped her hands. "Lois! I'd recognize you anywhere!" She picked up a hat from the counter beside her. "And look what I found to go with it."

"Oh, Mom, I don't know." Laurie took the hat dubiously and turned toward the mirror. It was a small black felt hat that perched at the front of her head. The short veil came down almost to the tip of her nose. Laurie shook her head as she took it off again. "Sorry, Mom, I just can't. I'd feel too stupid."

"Okay. Then let's go have some lunch on the way home. I'm hungry."

An hour later the two of them were in Laurie's mother's apartment. Laurie's mom was on her knees pawing through a box. "Aha!" she said triumphantly. "I knew there was a reason I held on to these." She held up a pair of shoes for Laurie's inspection.

They were suede, in a darker plum color than the dress, and they were held on by straps that crossed at the back and buckled at the front of the ankle. But the most amazing part was the heels. To Laurie's eyes they looked about four inches tall.

Laurie gazed at the shoes and then turned to her mother in astonishment. "You wore these, Mom?"

"Sure, honey," her mom replied with a laugh. "I wasn't always grown-up and sensible. In my day everybody had these Joan Crawford–style shoes. Of course, mine aren't from the forties, but these styles do keep on coming back over and over. Go ahead, Laurie, try them on."

Sliding her feet into the shoes, Laurie fastened the buckles and stood up. She felt about six feet tall, but the shoes were surprisingly comfortable. When she walked across the room, though, she nearly tripped. The straps and the unfamiliar height of the heels threw her a little off balance.

Laurie looked at her mom. "I guess I need to practice walking in these. But they fit perfectly. Are you sure it's okay for me to borrow them?"

Her mother grinned. "I wasn't planning to wear them anytime soon. Of course it's okay, I'm happy you have an excuse to wear them."

"Great," Laurie said. "Thanks, a lot, Mom." She thought it was a stroke of luck that her feet were the same size as her mom's, and an even bigger stroke of luck that the shoes had been packed away and not thrown out. Laurie hadn't even known that ankle straps were the right look for the forties. It was nice that her mom had gotten so involved in creating a Lois Lane costume.

But what was she going to do about a hairstyle to continue the Lois Lane look? Unconsciously she ran a hand through her long straight hair—it definitely needed help.

"Mom?" Her mother glanced up, and Laurie said hesitantly, "What do you think I should do with my hair?"

Anna Carr looked at her daughter thoughtfully. "I was wondering about that earlier. It's the right length for a Rita Hayworth style—you know, parted on one side with loose waves and curls around your face."

Laurie was already shaking her head in dismay. "Curls, Mom? You know how my hair is. They'd last about thirty seconds."

"Well, you'd have to use an awful lot of setting gel and spray, but I think it might hold for one evening." She paused, and then went on almost shyly, "I still have a curling iron around somewhere. Would you like to give it a try?"

When Laurie returned from the drugstore with an assortment of hair products and the barrette Mom had reminded her to get, the curling iron was heating up. Laurie sat in front of a mirror with a towel around her shoulders to catch drips of hair gel. Her eyes followed Anna Carr's hands as she deftly shaped Laurie's goopy hair into waves and fat curls held in place with bobby pins. As soon as the gel had dried, her mother carefully removed the pins and took out a brush. Using the curling iron, she gently wound the stray hairs into the mass of cascading curls and fastened a barrette into a wave on one side.

"Close your eyes and put your hands over your face," Mom said. "I'm going to use a lot of this spray."

At last Laurie felt the towel being whisked away from her shoulders. "Okay, honey, how do you like it?"

She stared at herself in amazement. She might have posed for one of those movie pictures in the old book she and Amy had paged through one night. Grinning at her mom in the mirror, Laurie exclaimed, "Wow, it's fabulous!" Impulsively she jumped up and threw her arms around her mother in a hug. "Oh, Mom, thanks!"

"You don't have to thank me, honey, I loved doing it." Her mom's voice sounded a little shaky as she hugged Laurie close. Standing there in her mother's embrace, Laurie thought how good it felt.

CHAPTER 13

LAURIE PUT A HAND UP TO TOUCH THE unfamiliar waves that framed her face. They felt as if they'd been starched, but they still looked great. She just hoped the curls would last until the end of the party.

She turned to look at the lines she'd drawn up the backs of her legs with eyebrow pencil—neither she nor her mother owned any stockings with seams. Then Laurie's father called to her up the stairs. "Laurie, Mark is here!"

It wasn't easy to walk in the unaccustomed high-heeled shoes, but Laurie managed to get downstairs without tripping. Then she saw Mark and began to laugh. "Oh, Superman, you look fabulous!"

His belted Clark Kent trench coat hung open to reveal his Superman costume—a tight long-sleeved blue T-shirt with Superman's emblem painted on it in slightly runny red and yellow. His legs were encased in what looked like blue elasticized running tights, and he wore a red swimsuit topped with a heavy black belt to complete the image. It all looked a bit mismatched up close, but Mark had obviously put a lot of energy into his outfit.

Laurie had wondered what he would do about his feet—after all, it couldn't be so easy to find red Superman-type boots. But Mark wore what looked like an old pair of cowboy boots, covered with red sports socks. They looked a bit peculiar, but they were definitely red.

He followed her glance at the boots. "I just hope these socks won't start to shred too early—I'd like to impress everyone with the total effect first."

"Well, I'm definitely impressed," she told him. "And I love your hair!" He had slicked back his unruly dark hair with some kind of shiny goo, and had used the same stuff to form Superman's trademark curl in the middle of his forehead. It looked absurd, but Mark clearly didn't care.

He grinned at Laurie. "Your hair looks pretty good, too. In fact, the whole outfit is stunning. If Superman were the type to wolf-whistle, I'd certainly whistle. Come on, Lois, let's go get that story for the *Daily Planet*!"

Laurie kissed her father and followed Mark out the door. As she stepped carefully into the car, pulling the calf-length skirt out of the way of the closing door, she thought that Mark wasn't quite as handsome as the heroic Superman. But his face was always alive with intelligence and humor, and Laurie thought, That matters much more than traditional good looks.

As Mark drove slowly along Amy's street looking for a parking place, Laurie saw Chuck's Jeep at the curb. For a moment her heart sank and she wished Amy hadn't invited him. But he was sort of a friend of Richard's, and after all, Laurie told herself, what difference does it make? He'll ignore you and you'll ignore him and everything will be fine.

The minute they got inside Amy's house, Tim and Billy grabbed them. "Come on, Laurie, you guys have to go through our haunted house before you can do anything else!"

Obediently Laurie and Mark trooped down to the basement and allowed the boys to blindfold them. Billy took Laurie's hand and led her through a doorway. Though she was prepared for all kinds of gimmicks, Laurie jumped when something brushed against her face. "That's the cobweb made by the spiders of the haunted house," Billy intoned solemnly. "They spin their webs to guard the secrets of Momo, the mad murderer!"

Guiding her between what felt like card tables, the little boy took her hand. "Momo likes to dissect his victims' brains," he said, plunging Laurie's hand into a slimy-feeling mess. Though she knew it was cold spaghetti or something similar, Laurie couldn't help gasping and snatching her hand back quickly. Billy giggled delightedly and moved her along to the next exhibit. Meanwhile Laurie could hear Tim telling Mark about the cobweb as they entered the haunted house.

The last stop was a chance to shake hands with Momo himself. Laurie braced herself, but it wasn't too bad—she guessed it was a rubber glove filled with ice that Billy put into her outstretched right hand. Then he took her through the doorway and untied her blindfold.

"Wow, that was really scary, Billy," she told him.

"Yeah, it's pretty good," he said proudly. "You were scared to touch the brains, weren't you?"

"I was scared to touch *everything,*" Laurie assured him, and Billy smiled with pleasure.

Then Mark emerged from the haunted house and the two of them went upstairs to join the party. Twenty or more costumed teenagers seemed to fill the living room of Amy's house to overflowing, and Laurie looked around for her friend. Amy looked fabulous in a flowing silky turquoise gown and a purple velvet turban that completely concealed her blond curls. Turquoise eye shadow and black eyeliner gave her eyes a melodramatic intensity, and it was a bit surprising to hear Amy's ordinary voice emerge from her red-lipsticked mouth.

"Oh, you guys look terrific! I *love* that dress, Laurie, you should keep it to wear for real later on; it looks great on you. And your makeup is perfect—just like all those old pictures out of *Life* magazine."

"Thanks," Laurie said, "you look fabulous yourself."

Amy glanced at the crowd spilling noisily through the living-room doorway into the hall. "Everybody seems kind of hyper," she said with a little frown. "Richard wants us all to go trick-or-treating, just to get the good out of these costumes, but I don't know. What do you think?"

"I think it's a good idea," Mark told her. "It'll be fun and then we can come back here and do whatever you have in mind."

"Eat," Amy told him with a grin. "My mom made enough food for an army, so I hope everyone will be hungry." She turned to Richard, who had come up behind her in a scarecrow costume with real straw poking out of the sleeves. "Get everyone organized—we're going trick-or-treating," she said.

"Great! Got any goodie bags for all the treats?"

Amy found a bunch of grocery bags in the kitchen and soon she was standing by the front door, handing one to each person as the group filed outside.

Soon a weird collection of vampires, werewolves, and medieval princesses was tramping along the sidewalk, exchanging "Happy Halloweens!" with children in costumes. At each house the people looked surprised to see a bunch of tall teenagers at the door, but they good-naturedly handed out candy and gum and, at one house on the corner, plastic Halloween favors. Laurie slipped a black bat ring on her little finger (the only one it would fit) and laughed as Richard carried on his running evaluation of all the jack-o'-lanterns they passed.

"Too complicated and artsy," he complained about one with star-shaped eyes. "Jack-o'-lanterns should be both traditional *and* creative, like that one." He pointed to a tall skinny pumpkin whose triangular eyes and jagged teeth seemed to scowl menacingly into the night. "That one's an A-plus."

"No, the eyes are uneven," Sean argued. "We have to maintain our standards of perfection here."

Their little group had lagged behind the others, and now up ahead Laurie saw Chuck swoop dramatically around the corner toward two little boys. Chuck had come as Dracula, and his flowing black cape and painted eyebrows and mustache made him a dramatically evil figure. One of the boys began to cry in fear as Chuck swirled the cape over his head and said in a cruel voice, "Aha! What have we here?" Laurie heard Meryl's high-pitched giggle as she and Chuck walked on, surrounded by a small group of admiring friends.

Angrily Laurie muttered to Amy, "That jerk! You shouldn't have invited him." Then she walked quickly toward the two children. Bending down, she said, "Don't be scared, he's just showing off."

The child sniffled. “I know,” he said shakily. “But I want to go home.”

“Where do you live?” Laurie asked.

He pointed to a house across the street, and the other boy said, “It’s okay, we gotta go inside now anyway.”

Laurie and the others watched as the two boys paused dutifully at the curb to look for cars and then ran across the street and up to a house whose lights were burning brightly.

Then they all walked on, but the fun had gone out of the trick-or-treating for Laurie, and she was glad when they came around the block and returned to Amy’s house.

Everyone swarmed around the table where apple cider and hot dogs and all sorts of snacks had been set out. Laurie and Mark retreated to the stairway, which was the only place left to sit down. Sinking as gracefully as she could onto the lowest step, Laurie thought, These shoes aren’t as comfortable as I thought at first.

Over the roar of talk and laughter, which seemed even louder now than before, Mark said ruefully, “Can’t walk many more miles in these boots. Now I know why Superman always flew.” He held out one foot, and Laurie saw that the red sock was held together across the bottom by only a few threads.

Amy leaned against the staircase. “I’m so happy everyone wore costumes,” she said, “I was afraid people might fink out and just wear regular clothes.”

Laurie glanced at the crowd in the living room. "Looks like everybody really got into the Halloween spirit."

Amy looked at Mark. "I think your Superman outfit is fabulous, Mark—but where's your cape?"

"I forgot about a cape," Mark said, smacking his forehead with one hand. "I had that trench coat for the Clark Kent part of the costume, but it's so warm in here, I had to take it off."

"Well, you need a cape," Amy said decisively. "And I know just what you can use. Mom has this old red plastic tablecloth for picnics in the summer and I think it's down in the basement somewhere. It's already ripped, so she probably won't mind if we cut it up to make a cape. Come on, let's go get it." Amy dragged Mark off toward the kitchen, and Laurie stood up to go and get more cider.

It was very warm in the house. Clutching her full cup of cider, Laurie moved toward the open bay window. Too late she noticed Chuck and Meryl standing partly hidden by the long drapes. She stopped short.

"What's the matter, Laurie?" Chuck's voice was mocking. "I don't think you're wearing the right costume for spying on other people."

Meryl giggled. "Not the right shoes, either," she said, gazing adoringly at Chuck.

Laurie was about to turn away, but Chuck added, "Not that you'd be much good as a spy anyway—you're too goody-goody for that, aren't you?"

Why couldn't he just leave her alone? Angrily Laurie replied, "Maybe I am, but I'd rather be a goody-goody, as you call it, than an underhanded cheat who just uses other people."

Chuck stared hard at her, his mocking smile replaced with a stony look. "What do you mean?" he asked softly.

Laurie stared back at him. She remembered guiltily that Mr. Gordon had asked her and Millie not to talk about the stolen history test. She shouldn't have even responded to Chuck's nasty comments. Finally she muttered, "Forget it, it's not important."

Gratefully Laurie saw that Angela, whose witch's hat kept banging into things whenever she moved too quickly, was standing at the food table refilling her plate with taco chips and pretzels. She moved toward the other girl and the two of them fell into a conversation about favorite Halloween costumes they'd worn when they were little. Sean joined them and sent them into gales of laughter as he described the television set complete with antenna he'd constructed when he was nine.

"Now it would have to be a computer, Sean," Angela teased.

Just then Tim and Billy walked through the room, heading for the kitchen. Their trick-or-treat sacks looked heavily laden with goodies, and they stopped to give Laurie and the others a glimpse of the loot they'd collected.

"I'm trading all my candy corn to Tim, 'cause I hate it," Billy announced.

"I hate it, too," Laurie told him. "Lucky for you Tim likes it."

"Hey, you guys, that was a great haunted house you set up in the basement." Richard had wandered over to join them.

"Yeah, but next year we're gonna do one even better, in the whole house, not just the basement." Tim's enthusiasm made them smile.

As the two boys continued into the kitchen Sean said, "I always loved haunted houses."

Richard nodded. "Me, too. There was a big house down the street from us that I always thought a witch lived in."

Sean looked thoughtful. "You know, there's a house near here that's really spooky looking. I bet it's the neighborhood haunted house."

Laurie felt a shiver run down her spine. She knew which house Sean was talking about—it was the one the child's voice had led her to on that gray afternoon.

CHAPTER 14

"NO KIDDING?" RICHARD SOUNDED FAScinated. "A haunted house somewhere right around here. Where is it?"

"Oh, a couple blocks over that way." Sean gestured vaguely with one arm. "I used to go past it when I went to my piano lesson every week. It's got this iron fence, you know, the kind with the pointed tops, only it's all rusty. And there are these big old trees that kind of hide the house. I always used to walk on the other side of the street from it when I was younger so if anybody saw me checking it out, I could run away. But I never saw anyone there except once, when this creepy-looking guy was unlocking the front door to go in. I tried to see inside a bunch of times, but the windows were always covered up."

With every word Sean said, Laurie felt colder. Her heart was thumping painfully in her chest. She wished Sean would stop talking about the house.

But Richard was full of enthusiasm. "Hey,

that's cool!" he exclaimed. "Maybe there's a secret bomb factory inside, or a transmitter sending messages to alien planets! Of course, it might just be your standard run-of-the-mill haunted house." He made a face of mock disappointment.

By this time several other people were listening. Bob Green chimed in, "Nah, it's probably just a hideout where the mass murderer chops up the bodies." Behind him someone squealed in pretend horror. Bob lowered his voice to an ominous whisper. "And Halloween night is when he roams the world looking for fresh victims!"

"I say we go check it out, and see what's inside. Then we can lay these vicious rumors to rest once and for all." Richard raised his hand over his head and gestured wildly while bits of straw fluttered to the floor. "Onward, to the haunted house!"

"Onward!" Someone else echoed the cry. Soon it seemed to Laurie that the whole room was urging a mass invasion of the spooky old house.

Laurie stood stock-still, silent and trembling. Were they really going to go to the old house? The idea terrified her. And where was Mark? She needed to feel his comforting presence. But in a lull in the noise she could hear Mark's voice coming from the kitchen. It sounded as if he was explaining something about the ozone layer.

Laurie looked around. People were laughing

and talking, and no one actually seemed to be moving toward the door to go to the haunted house—at least not yet. But the room was full of pent-up energy and she thought that any minute the whole group might surge out the door and down the street. And then what? Laurie shuddered.

Behind her Chuck said, "What's the matter, Laurie? You look upset. Don't you want to go investigate the haunted house?"

He was standing very close to her, leaning down to almost whisper the words in her ear. Shaking her head, Laurie said, "No!"

"But why not?" Chuck was still speaking softly, almost intimately, but Laurie could hear the mockery beneath his words. "There's nothing to be afraid of, not if big brave Mark comes along to protect you. But, oh—I forgot!" He tilted her chin up with one finger and smiled at her. "You can't do anything unless your voices tell you to, right?"

What made him think that her voices had anything to do with that house? A cold wave of fear mingled with anger washed over Laurie. Unable to move, she stared back at Chuck. His Dracula makeup made his smirk even more diabolic.

Enjoying himself, Chuck kept talking. "It must be hard to know what those voices want, Laurie. What are they telling you right now?"

He paused for a moment. In that brief space of time a muffled roaring filled Laurie's ears.

Through it she could just hear a faint little voice. "Please, somebody help me." The despairing words clutched at her heart. No, please no, she begged silently.

"I know what we'll do," Chuck was saying. "We'll have a little seance. Isn't that what you people call it? And we'll get everybody to help you find out what your voices are telling you." He took hold of her shoulder with one hand. "Hey, everyone, listen up, we've got to help Laurie."

In a panic Laurie tore herself out of his grasp. Tears of angry humiliation welled up in her eyes and spilled down her cheeks. How could he be so cruel? She felt that everyone in the room was staring at her, some with concern but most with a kind of ghoulish glee. She was alone, surrounded by Chuck's mocking laughter.

Running toward the door, Laurie nearly fell as one of the ungainly high-heeled shoes slipped under her foot. A brief wrench of pain shot through her ankle, but she kept going, yanking open the front door and escaping finally into the night.

It was darker now, and the street was empty. Laurie stumbled out to the sidewalk still trembling uncontrollably and brushing away the tears that filled her eyes again.

"Please, please help me!" The little voice was clearer now, and it sounded more hopeless than ever. What was she going to do?

Walking blindly down the sidewalk, Laurie

couldn't seem to think coherently about anything. The only thing she knew was that she just had to get away.

"Laurie! Wait!"

Limping slightly, she tried to walk faster, but running footsteps caught up to her. "Laurie, what's the matter?" Mark caught her arm and turned her to face him.

His face was full of worried concern, but Laurie was beyond all that. Great waves of anger and fear still clouded her mind, making it impossible to focus on anything but her humiliation and her determination somehow to prove herself—she wasn't sure to whom or how.

Laurie shook off Mark's hand. "Just leave me alone." Every word was bitten off, sharp and cold.

Mark looked astonished. "But what is it? Angela told me you just ran out of the house without saying a word to anyone." He paused, but Laurie didn't reply. "Did I do something?" His voice was insistent. "What's wrong?"

"Just go away, Mark." The vehemence in her tone almost frightened Laurie. But it seemed to get through to him.

He gazed at her for a long moment. "Well, okay, I guess you're mad about something, but at least let me drive you home."

"Leave me alone!" She spaced the words to give each one emphasis, in a voice that was harsh and strange to her ears.

Mark stepped back, holding up his hands in

surrender. "Okay, okay, Laurie. Whatever you say. I just wish I understood what's going on with you."

Laurie couldn't stand to look any longer at the puzzled hurt in his face. She wished she could explain that she wasn't really mad at him. But she didn't seem to understand anything anymore. It was as if the voice had control over her, as if she no longer had a mind of her own. She shook her head as if to clear it and then turned her back on Mark and walked away down the sidewalk.

"Please help me. Please." The last word was drawn out in a sob. For the first time Laurie almost welcomed the sound. The voice was coming from the direction of the old house—the "haunted house." She could feel it pulling at her. And now she knew what she had to do. She would let the voice lead her on to the end this time. She wouldn't let anything stop her.

Clouds drifted across the moon, shadowing its watery gleam as Laurie moved like a sleepwalker along the sidewalk. She crossed the street and turned the corner. A jack-o'-lantern on a front porch flickered and went out. With part of her mind she heard the creak of branches as the wind came in a sudden gust, showering her with the last of autumn's dry leaves.

Across the street from the house with the iron fence, Laurie stopped. Her stomach twisted, perhaps from nervous excitement, perhaps from fear. There was no car in the cracked and overgrown driveway, and the house looked completely dark—no light showed around the edges of the windows. Yet, more than ever, Laurie felt sure the voice was leading her into that strange old house.

She stood hesitating, glancing over her shoulder. The wind had risen and leaves blew in little whirls across the sidewalk. The branches of the tall evergreens in the yard across the street whipped back and forth in the gusts, banging into the house every now and then with small dull thuds.

I must be crazy, she thought, suddenly grasping what she was about to do. I can't just go up to the door and explain that someone is calling me from this house—and besides, it looks like there's no one home. She half turned away and took a step toward the main street; there would be lights, people, traffic, all the normal things of life.

"Oh, please, won't somebody help?"

Like an iron bolt drawn by a magnet, Laurie was pulled back toward the house. It was no use fighting it. She'd known all along that she'd have to follow the child's voice as far as she could. With a shudder, she thought, It's not real, because no one is home in that place.

But she knew it didn't matter. Whatever it was, she'd come too far to turn back now. Squaring her shoulders, Laurie walked across the street and stared for a moment at the shuttered house. Its closed doors and tightly covered windows gave it the look of a blind creature turned in on itself, hostile and ready to lash out at any intruder.

Warily Laurie stretched out her hand and pushed the tall iron gate that hung from rusted hinges. They creaked ominously, making her jump. She waited a moment, but no one appeared. Gathering her courage, she stepped through the opening and walked, knees trembling, up to the front door.

The doorbell dangled from a broken, twisted piece of wire; it obviously hadn't worked for ages. Taking a deep breath, Laurie cast one more glance down the empty street. Then she knocked loudly three times on the door.

Waiting there on the front step was almost the hardest thing Laurie had ever done. She felt exposed. What if someone did answer the door? Or even worse, what if someone saw her from the sidewalk and asked what she thought she was doing? Laurie wrapped her arms around herself, feeling sweaty and chilled at the same time. By now, she thought, if anyone was home, they'd have answered the door. But it would be stupid not to make sure. Laurie knocked again and waited, straining to hear any noise behind the door. But the house remained silent as death.

At last she turned and walked back down the steps. Her arms and legs felt stiff, full of unreleased tension that made her muscles ache.

She'd done everything she could. Now she would just go home and take a shower and fall into bed.

But even as she thought this Laurie knew she wouldn't do it. Without consciously willing it, she found herself walking slowly around the side of the house. Pushing aside the overgrown evergreen branches that slapped at her face, she realized how isolated the old house was. The small bungalow next door was at the far side of the property, and the thick trees and a hedge behind them made a living wall that looked impenetrable.

At the back the house looked even more run-down than in front. Paint had chipped and peeled off the wooden sides, and the porch railing was broken, its slats sticking out at crazy angles. No light shone from inside. Why am I doing this? Laurie asked herself. But as she formed this rational, sensible thought she was climbing carefully up the back stairs to the porch.

Cautiously she tried the doorknob of the back door. It was firmly locked, as she'd expected. But there were two windows that looked onto the porch, and one of them had a cracked pane.

Going closer to look at it, Laurie saw that the window itself was crooked in its frame. Maybe it wasn't latched. Gently at first, she tried to push the bottom half up. She felt it give slightly and pushed harder. Suddenly the window seemed to straighten in the wooden frame. It slid smoothly all the way open.

Laurie stood on the rickety porch, staring through the window into the dark room beyond. This is it, she thought. Now or never. All sorts of unrelated phrases spun through her mind—breaking and entering, scaredy-cat, haunted house, you can't do anything unless your voices tell you to, get off this property and never come back. But stronger than any of these was the piteous plea she now heard again: "Please help me."

Laurie swallowed hard and wiped her clammy hands on her skirt. Then, with a final look around the dark yard, she pulled herself with shaking hands up onto the windowsill and crawled through into the house.

CHAPTER 15

IT WAS DARK INSIDE, WITH ONLY A FEW thin moonbeams making their way through the overgrown trees outside, but Laurie could see that she was in a kitchen. A table with four mismatched wooden chairs stood near the window, and as she swung down to the floor the heel of one of her shoes banged against a chair.

Laurie froze, but nothing moved or made a noise inside the house. After a few moments she let out the breath she'd been holding and looked around her. It was hard to see much, but even in the dimness the kitchen looked barren and cold. Laurie thought it wasn't a place where people spent happy times together. She shivered slightly and began to move quietly across the room to the doorway beyond.

Prowling through the hallway, and the living room and dining room that opened off it, Laurie thought, Maybe no one lives here. There was so little furniture—only a bookcase, nearly empty, in the dining room, and in the living room a sagging couch and an ancient, tiny television on a ratty wicker stand.

But someone had been living here last spring, she remembered, because that was when Amy's brother Tim had met the mean man who told him to leave. Immediately Laurie was sorry she'd remembered this. What if that horrible man still lived here? He might come home any minute, and what would he do if he found her in his house?

For a moment Laurie felt a nearly irresistible urge to run out of the house, to put as much distance as she could between herself and the possibility of meeting up with a man who sounded truly scary. But at the same time she felt compelled to stay, to go back to the kitchen.

As if in a trance, Laurie moved through the kitchen doorway and stood in the middle of the room. Now she saw a door that she hadn't noticed before. The same compulsion that had drawn her back to the kitchen pulled her toward this door. Without even deciding to do it, she reached out her hand and opened it.

The faint moonlight that filtered into the kitchen allowed Laurie to see that beyond the door was a staircase leading down to the basement. And she didn't want to go down those stairs. The idea of descending into that cold, sinister cellar filled her with terror; it was like lowering herself into a tomb. Yet she knew she had to.

She brushed her hand over the walls just

inside the doorway, looking for a light switch, but she couldn't find one. Laurie hovered irresolute for a moment at the top of the staircase—it was crazy to go down there! Then, step by careful step, one hand on the wall beside her, she crept down into the darkness.

And then she heard it—not calling or crying out this time, just sobbing hopelessly. It was a child weeping, and Laurie felt absolutely certain that it was the child who'd been calling to her these past weeks. But this child was real—the sniffles and gulps could only belong to a living human being. Laurie almost staggered as a tremendous wave of relief engulfed her. She wasn't totally crazy, she hadn't been hearing voices from another planet, she'd somehow been hearing a real live kid. He was somewhere in the basement of this house, and she was determined to find him.

Continuing carefully down the flight of narrow stairs, Laurie stopped at the bottom. She could see a little better now, and in a moment she found the reason: a night-light in the shape of Donald Duck shone dimly from a socket on the wall near her. In its feeble glow Laurie could see that the basement was full of the kind of junk that collects in basements everywhere. A broken bed frame topped by a mattress full of holes, boxes stacked in precarious piles that reached almost to the low ceiling, a tall wooden dresser missing two of its five drawers, and heaps of smaller things that were impossible to identify.

On the other side of the large room Laurie could see a door. She could still hear the child's crying, quieter and slower now. Was the crying coming from behind the door? She thought it was. Stepping cautiously, she began to make her way across the cluttered space toward it. As she got closer she could make out a big bolt that held the door shut.

Laurie quickened her pace, and then abruptly stopped dead. What was that noise? In a moment she heard it again—someone was walking with heavy footsteps in the kitchen above her head! As she stood there immobilized with fear the footsteps began to descend the staircase.

Frantically Laurie's eyes searched the heaps of junk that cluttered the basement. Where could she hide? There wasn't much time to decide, and in a moment she had darted behind one of the massive square brick pillars that supported the ceiling and the floor above it. Her heart was pounding wildly and her breath came in little gasps. What if he heard her?

The man who was coming down the stairs now appeared in Laurie's view. The light was too dim for her to see whether he was young or old, but he moved in a solid, purposeful way. In one hand he held something flat that looked like a plate or a pie pan.

Terrified and trying to hold herself absolutely

still, Laurie watched around the edge of the pillar as the man walked toward the bolted door. He bent down to set whatever he was carrying on the floor. Then he stood straight again and reached for the bolt on the door with both hands.

Laurie craned her neck to see what would happen when he opened the door. The crying had stopped, as if the child had heard the man's footsteps. But who was the child behind the door? She had to find out.

Perhaps she could risk looking around the pillar just a little bit to get a better view of the door. Holding on to the solid column of brick with one arm, she leaned sideways. But the unaccustomed high heels she wore were treacherous, and the ankle she'd twisted at Amy's house buckled under her again.

Instinctively Laurie flung out her arm to catch herself. She didn't fall, but her flailing arm hit the decrepit chest of drawers, and it rocked noisily on its uneven legs.

The man whirled around and stared into the dim room. "Who's there?" His voice was sharp and angry.

Laurie stood behind the wide pillar, her hand pressed to her mouth and her eyes opened wide in fear. The two of them remained frozen for a long moment, held motionless and silent in the darkness.

Then she heard a soft sound—he must have bent down to push the object he'd set on the floor almost noiselessly out of his way. There was another long moment of almost unbearable silence. Had he moved? Laurie couldn't tell. She clutched one hand with the other, and something dug into her palm. It was the plastic bat ring she'd slipped onto her little finger when she'd been trick-or-treating with Mark—it seemed like a lifetime ago.

A faint sound reached her ears and her hands clenched even more tightly together. What was the man doing? Concealed behind the pillar, Laurie could no longer see him, but she knew he must have moved away from the bolted door. Was he coming in her direction?

She heard a click; there was probably a light switch down here somewhere, and he had tried to turn it on. Thank God it hadn't worked—the bulb must have burned out. But now she could hear a slight brushing sound. She racked her brain to identify it. She heard it once more and then she knew. It was the whispery noise made by a person's pants legs brushing against one another as he walked.

What should she do? In a panic, Laurie raked the crowded room with her eyes, searching desperately for another hiding place. Not the dresser—it was too close to where she was standing now, and besides, the man might have realized what had made the sound that alerted him.

But beyond the dresser were those stacks of boxes. They were tall enough to conceal a standing person. Laurie shuddered; it was impossible to imagine crouching down to hide behind anything that was lower to the ground. She would feel too vulnerable, too exposed.

Too late Laurie wished she had thought of taking off the stupid shoes. No matter how hard she tried to move silently, the clicking of their heels on the concrete floor would give her away. And she certainly couldn't run fast in them. Even if she could manage to reach the stairs ahead of him, he'd catch her before she got to the top. But she couldn't take time now to bend down and unfasten those little buckles that held the straps locked around her ankles.

There was a bumping noise. "Damn!" The word was muttered under the man's breath. He must have bumped into the old bed frame that stood between him and Laurie. That meant he was getting closer. She had to move!

Fearfully, cautiously, Laurie edged around the dresser that was in back of her, putting it between herself and the place she thought the man had reached. Now there was open space to cross before she could hide behind the boxes. She didn't think she could force her legs to carry her across it. But there were no other choices left.

Gathering her courage, Laurie took three quick steps. Then she was behind the boxes, trembling from head to foot with tension and fear. But she thought he couldn't have heard her—she'd put her feet down carefully so the shoes wouldn't make any noise, and the fabric of the jersey dress she wore made no sound at all as she moved.

She strained her ears; the brushing sound was nearer. It was the only thing that betrayed his presence as he looked behind the pillar and the dresser. Which way would he move next? Trapped, Laurie wondered desperately, Where can I go now?

Another pile of boxes loomed a few feet away, nearer to the bolted door. But it was in the wrong direction. She needed to get to the stairs, or at least to the night-light so she could turn it off and make it harder for the man to see her.

The basement was totally silent now. No sound at all reached Laurie where she stood barely breathing behind her stack of cardboard boxes. What was the man doing? Was he waiting for her to move, to panic and reveal her hiding place? Maybe he knew exactly where she was by this time. He could be toying with her, hoping she'd lose control and make a wild run for the stairs and safety. Her hands clenched into fists as she begged her body to remain motionless.

The silence stretched out until Laurie could hardly stand it. She was like a rabbit cowering in a hole, hoping against hope that the ravening dogs wouldn't find her. She thought she might scream, just to bring this unbearable hunt to an end. Don't do it! she told herself fiercely. She brought her hand to her face and bit down hard on the knuckle of her index finger, willing herself not to make a sound.

And then it began again—the stealthy rustling that meant the man was on the move. This time Laurie knew there was no hope. There was no other hiding place she could reach without betraying to him where she was. And she had no chance of making it to the stairs before he caught her, not in that cluttered space and not with those horrible shoes that would trip her again in a minute.

But she had to try. Anything was better than waiting to be caught like a mouse in a trap. She'd wait until the man got even nearer to where she hid, even though every muscle of her body urged her to run while there was still time to get away. Then she'd push the stack of boxes at him, hoping the crash would confuse him and the fallen boxes would at least delay his pursuit.

Her jaw tightened as Laurie set her hands against the boxes, ready to shove them hard toward the sinister sound that was creeping ever closer to her.

"Laurie? Laurie, where are you?"

It was Mark's voice, echoing down the stairs from the kitchen on the first floor! Laurie's pulse began to race faster than before. Then Mark's footsteps began to clomp down the narrow staircase.

"Are you down here, Laurie?" His voice sounded louder than before. Now Laurie heard the man in the basement moving quickly toward the stairs.

"Mark! Watch out! He's going to—"

In a spasm of anxiety, Laurie pushed her hands convulsively against the insecurely balanced stack of boxes, and they tumbled to the floor with a noisy crash. Startled, the man glanced quickly back over his shoulder. Then he turned again toward the stairs.

Alerted by Laurie's shouted warning, Mark faced the man from the next-to-last step. As the man reached for him Mark tried to kick him away, but the man was much stronger than he was. Ignoring Mark's kick, the man tried to hit him, but the narrow space made it impossible.

With a yell of rage, the man grabbed Mark's arm and pulled him off the steps. Losing his balance, Mark stumbled heavily against the man's shoulder, and both of them fell to the floor.

Her heart in her mouth, Laurie raced awkwardly across the room. The man was already on top of Mark, trying to pound his head against the concrete floor. He was going to kill him!

"Stop! Stop!" Laurie yelled, but of course her words went unheard. The man's frenzy seemed to grow stronger as she watched in horror. How could she stop him?

A heap of old junk lay against the wall near the stairs. Something long and thin was visible—was it a broom? Laurie took two quick steps and yanked it out of the pile. It was an old garden spade, with a heavy blade and a sturdy round handle.

Laurie turned and saw Mark's bent knees banging frantically against the man's body, trying to dislodge him. But the man didn't seem to feel the blows. He was totally focused on pounding Mark into unconsciousness against the unyielding floor, and Laurie knew that any moment he would succeed.

She had never hit anyone before in her life. But with a strength and determination she didn't know she possessed, Laurie raised the spade by its handle and swung the blade hard against the back of the man's head.

In horrifying slow motion, he dropped his hands from Mark's shoulders and lifted his head. For a moment he seemed to stare straight at Laurie. Then his eyes rolled back in his head and he toppled slowly sideways. His heavyset body made a soft thudding noise on the concrete, and he lay crumpled and still at her feet.

Laurie dropped the spade with a clatter and stood staring at the man. Had she actually hit him? She could hardly believe it. She wondered with a sick feeling in her stomach if she had hit him too hard. What if he was dead?

The only sound was Mark's breathing, coming in quick panting gasps. Then at last he moved, pushing the man's body away and climbing slowly to his feet.

Laurie ran to him and he rested one arm

heavily on her shoulder. "Mark, are you all right?" Her voice was shaking.

Mark shook his head experimentally. "Yeah, I think so," he told her, "but I'm gonna have a headache for quite a while." He looked down at the man. "What did you do to this guy?"

"I hit him with that." Laurie gestured at the spade on the floor. "Mark, do you think I killed him?" She couldn't control her breath, and the words came out in short bursts.

"No," Mark told her, "I can see that he's breathing." Laurie looked where he pointed and then she, too, could see the man's chest moving up and down. "You just knocked him out." He smiled at her crookedly. "Lucky for me you did. But, Laurie, what were you doing down here in the first place?"

"Oh!" How could she have forgotten? She spoke rapidly, trying to explain everything as she dragged Mark over to the door with the heavy bolt. "There's a little kid—I heard him crying and so I came to look for him, and he's in here!"

"But, Laurie—" Mark began, but he broke off when he saw her anguished face. "Okay, let's open this door."

The bolt was big and it held the door tightly closed, but it slid easily in its track when Mark pushed it. Glancing at Laurie, Mark pulled the door wide open.

Another night-light, this time in the shape of Mickey Mouse, glowed on the wall of the little room. By the dim light it cast, Laurie and Mark could see a child seated on a flimsy canvas cot.

Laurie stood still for a moment in horror. The boy looked about seven years old, but he was so thin that his bones seemed about to poke through his skin. His longish dark hair was matted and tangled, and the ragged T-shirt he wore was much too small for him.

Slowly Laurie walked into the tiny room, which even in semidarkness looked filthy and uncared for. The child sat on the cot, clutching a thin, dirty blanket and staring back at Laurie with an expression she couldn't interpret.

"My God." Laurie heard Mark's low, shocked voice behind her. "What a horrible—Laurie, I'm going to find something to tie up our friend on the floor, and then I'm going to call the police."

Laurie nodded without taking her eyes off the child, who still watched her every move. Slowly she took another step toward him. "Don't be afraid," she told him quietly. "I'm not going to hurt you."

The little boy didn't say a word. He hadn't moved at all since they had opened the door to his room—or maybe she should think of it as his prison. Laurie felt she had to try to get some kind of response from this skinny, pathetic child. "My name is Laurie," she said softly. "What's your name?"

He stared at her for another long moment. Then he said in a tearful little voice that she recognized, "Please, Laurie, help me."

CHAPTER 16

LAURIE AND MARK SAT IN THE GRUBBY waiting room in the building that housed the county's Social Services Department. They'd been asked to come to the office and explain what had happened the night before, but so far they had seen only a harried-looking young man who told them to "Take a seat and wait for Ms. Kamisar."

Because it was Sunday, the building was nearly empty, and Laurie felt keyed up and nervous. Last night, while they waited for the police to arrive, she'd coaxed the little boy to tell her his name was Jimmy. She felt she had to get him out of that horrible little room; he shouldn't have to stay there a minute longer. But she'd had to carry him, and when he saw the man lying tied up on the floor, still unconscious, Jimmy had buried his head against her shoulder. She could feel his dreadfully thin body trembling all the way up the stairs.

When the police car and ambulance had finally arrived, Laurie was sitting on the lumpy couch in the living room with Jimmy on her lap. Mark let the patrolmen in and explained that the child had been locked up in a room in the basement, and the man who had locked him up was lying unconscious on the floor. Then he had led the ambulance driver and his helper down the stairs and watched while they maneuvered the man onto a stretcher.

Meanwhile a woman police officer had tried to take Jimmy off Laurie's lap. But the little boy had tightened his arms hard around Laurie's neck. He shook his head violently whenever the policewoman touched him. Finally she gave up and sat quietly talking to Laurie until another squad car arrived. Laurie had gone with Jimmy to the hospital, where he would spend at least that night while doctors checked to make sure he wasn't ill or hurt in some way they couldn't yet see.

After she surrendered Jimmy's fragile little body to a pleasant, motherly nurse, Laurie had had to go to the police station. When she walked in and saw Mark, Mark's parents, and her own father waiting for her, the terrifying events of the evening had caught up with her at last. Hot salty tears had begun streaming down her cheeks, and she was powerless to stop them.

The cops had been pretty nice, Laurie thought. They'd asked only a few questions to get the general idea of what had happened; Mark answered most of these questions while Laurie gulped and tried without much success to stop crying. Soon her dad had taken her home, with a promise that she would see the Social Services person the next day. So here she was.

"Mark Jacobs and Laurie Carr?"

Both of them looked up at the gray-haired woman who stood in the doorway of the inner office. She had a file in her hand and a tired look on her face, but when Laurie and Mark nodded, she smiled slightly and said, "I'm Rachel Kamisar. Please come in."

The desk and chairs in the small office were battered and clunky. But the yellow chrysanthemums in a vase on the desk formed a pool of cheerful color, and Laurie noticed a collection of dolls, trucks, and other toys on one of the lower shelves along the wall.

Rachel Kamisar followed Laurie's glance. "The kids who come in here to see me sometimes need time to play," she commented gently. When they had sat down, she took a small tape recorder out of her desk. "I'm going to be taping this interview," she said matter-of-factly. "Is that all right with you? It's just for my own information, so I don't have to write everything down while we talk."

Mark and Laurie both nodded a bit uncertainly. "Good," said Ms. Kamisar. She pushed a button on the little machine and Laurie could hear its faint hum come on. Then Rachel looked straight at Laurie. "Will you tell me exactly what happened last night, Laurie, that led to your finding Jimmy Stauffer locked up in the basement of his home?"

This was the moment Laurie had been dreading. How could she possibly explain to Ms. Kamisar, no matter how nice she seemed to be, that she had heard Jimmy's voice calling to her, and that his calls for help had led her to the old house and down to the basement? For Laurie was certain now that the voice had been Jimmy's.

She twined her hands together in her lap and flashed a look of desperate appeal at Mark. He smiled at her encouragingly, then reached over and took one of her hands in his own warm one. His touch steadied Laurie. She took a deep breath and began.

"Actually I have to start before last night," she said. She hoped her voice would stop shaking as she continued. "I had been hearing a voice for, oh, I guess about four weeks. It was a little kid's voice, and he kept crying out, 'Please help me.' I know it sounds totally weird and dumb, but this voice kept waking me up in the middle of the night, and it was always saying the same thing—'Help me, somebody please help me.'"

Rachel Kamisar's face expressed nothing but sympathetic interest. "How many times did you hear the voice call out?" she asked.

"Oh, about nine or ten times, I'm not exactly sure." Laurie's voice was more confident now. "Anyway, once when I heard it in the daytime, it sort of led me to that house—the one where we found Jimmy last night." Laurie couldn't help shuddering slightly at the memory. "But I didn't see him or anyone else there, and I had no idea who was calling to me or what I should do about it. I just wanted the voice to quit and leave me alone."

"Did you tell anyone about it?"

"Well, I was kind of scared to tell, because people would think I was totally crazy," Laurie answered slowly. She wouldn't mention telling Chuck unless she had to.

"Laurie told me about the voice." Mark sounded calm, and he gave Laurie's hand a quick squeeze. "She told me last weekend, and we tried to figure out who it was or what it meant."

"I see." Rachel looked back at Laurie. "So what happened last night?"

"There was a Halloween party at my friend Amy's house, which is pretty near the house where we found Jimmy," Laurie said. "And people were talking about that house, and saying it was weird and spooky and like a haunted house. They were saying they wanted to go and check it out. And that's when I started hearing Jimmy's voice again—at least, I didn't know then that it was Jimmy. But it sounded so sad and hopeless, and I just knew it was coming from that house. So I walked over there and I couldn't see any lights on inside. I knocked on the door, but no one came, so I went around to the back and—well, I guess you could say I broke in. I pushed a window open and climbed inside."

Laurie looked away from Ms. Kamisar's face. She somehow expected her to launch into a lecture about breaking into people's houses, but all the woman said was "And then what?"

"I looked all around the first floor of the house. And then, I don't know, something made me open the door to the basement and then I could hear Jimmy crying. I could tell it was a real kid crying down there, it wasn't like the voice I'd been hearing before, although it *was* the same voice—oh, I can't explain what I mean."

"I think you're making it very clear." Rachel Kamisar smiled at Laurie.

"Well, so I went down to the basement and I was walking toward the door of that room, because that's where I could hear the crying was. And then I heard someone walking in the kitchen and coming down the stairs. I was really scared, so I hid. Then I saw a man come downstairs and walk over to that door. He had something in his hand, but I couldn't see what it was."

"Yes." Rachel Kamisar looked at the folder that lay open on the desk in front of her. "The man's name is Ronald Stauffer. He was carrying a metal plate with a cheese sandwich on it."

"Oh." Somehow knowing the man's name made him seem more real to Laurie. "Well, I was trying to watch and see who was in that room when he opened the door, and I bumped into something and made a noise, and, um, Mr. Stauffer said, 'Who's there?' or something like that, and then he started walking over to find me. And I knew I couldn't let him catch me, so I hid behind something else, and I was going to push some stuff over at him and try to run upstairs. But then I heard Mark call to me and start coming down the stairs, and I yelled to him to watch out for the man. But they started fighting and the man—Mr. Stauffer—was on top of Mark and I was afraid he would kill him, he was so out of control. So I ran over and grabbed something that turned out to be a shovel, and I hit him with it."

It sounds pretty bad, Laurie thought. I wonder what they'll do to us. She had to make Ms. Kamisar understand that it wasn't Mark's fault at all—he'd only followed her into the house because he was worried about her.

"Thank you, Laurie, that's very clear." Rachel turned off the tape recorder and sat back in her chair. "I'm sure you have lots of questions, but first let me bring you up to date. Jimmy is still at the hospital. He's basically healthy, but he's somewhat malnourished and he's also very fearful and confused. He'll probably stay at the hospital for a few days and meanwhile we'll be finding a foster family that can take care of him."

"Can I go to see him?" Laurie hadn't meant to

break in, but the question came out before she thought.

Rachel Kamisar smiled. "I think so. I'll try to arrange it before you leave today." She glanced down at her folder and then went on. "Ronald Stauffer is Jimmy's uncle—that is, Jimmy is the illegitimate son of Ronald Stauffer's sister. And I don't want you to worry about Mr. Stauffer—he's fine, though I imagine his head hurts today."

She smiled again briefly at the two serious faces across the desk from her. Then, the smile fading from her pleasant features, she went on. "Jimmy's mother died about a year ago. According to Mr. Stauffer, his sister had learned a year before that she had stomach cancer, and she knew she wouldn't live very long." Mrs. Kamisar paused and then continued. "She never told who Jimmy's father was, and there weren't any other relatives. So, even though she and Mr. Stauffer had hardly spoken to each other for many years, she had no one else to turn to when she found out she was dying. Apparently she, and Mr. Stauffer too, felt strongly that people shouldn't be dependent on government services to do things for them. So she got in touch with her brother and expected him to take care of her child after she was gone."

Ms. Kamisar's face had a quizzical expression. "It's odd. Generally I'm all in favor of families taking care of their own and not expecting the government to help them out every time there's a problem. But in this case I think maybe Jimmy's mother carried that idea too far."

Mark frowned in a puzzled way. "Did you find out all this stuff just since last night?"

"Yes. I think it was a relief for Mr. Stauffer to talk about all this at last. My guess is that he's always been pretty much of a loner, someone who didn't want or need contact with other people. And so he found it almost impossible to deal with the normal demands of a young child. But at the same time, like his sister, he couldn't bring himself to ask for help from the government, or probably from anyone at all. He couldn't imagine putting the boy in foster care or finding some other place for him to live. I think he would have seen that as a bad reflection on himself, as proof that he was too weak to accept responsibility. So he was stuck."

Laurie shook her head slowly, her large brown eyes full of pain. "But Jimmy must be old enough to go to school, and there are lots of people who do child care after school. He wouldn't have even been around very much to bother Mr. Stauffer."

Nodding, Ms. Kamisar said, "I know. But I don't think Mr. Stauffer planned to send Jimmy to school; he seems to see it as another unwelcome intrusion by the government. So there he was, with a child he didn't want to have around but who he felt obligated to keep. My guess is that Mr. Stauffer doesn't like children in general and he seems to have been especially bothered by the fact that Jimmy is, as he puts it, a 'bastard.'"

"But that's not Jimmy's fault," Laurie said quietly.

"Of course not." Ms. Kamisar's blue eyes flashed briefly with indignation. "And in fact, it's pretty hard to untangle all the emotions that led Mr. Stauffer to behave the way he did. No doubt it was difficult for a single man who was used to being by himself to care for a little boy who had just lost his mother. In any case, Mr. Stauffer says that Jimmy cried a lot, and after a while he couldn't stand it, so one day he locked Jimmy in the basement to make him stop crying. And then I suspect it just seemed easier to him to shut the boy out of the way more and more of the time so he wouldn't have to deal with him."

"But that's terrible!" Mark burst out. "How could anyone do that to a little kid?"

Laurie couldn't speak. Her eyes wide in horror, she stared at the woman across the desk.

Rachel Kamisar sighed. "Yes, it is terrible. And what's frightening to all of us is that Jimmy was an 'invisible' child. No one knew that he was living here and that he should have been in school. He just fell through the holes in the safety net. People who knew Jimmy when he lived in Florida with his mother have apparently written to him once or twice but Mr.

Stauffer threw the letters away without answering them, and after a while the people gave up. The worst part is that even now I can't see how this whole situation could have been prevented—after all, the court couldn't very well keep Jimmy's only blood relative from having custody of him."

Shaking her head, Ms. Kamisar closed her folder with a snap. Then she folded her hands in front of her on the desk and gave Mark and Laurie a level stare. "Now, I can't tell the two of you that what you did was legal. You should, of course, have called the police and told them you suspected a child was being abused in that house. People can't take the law into their own hands as a general rule. However." She smiled at the two of them. "I don't believe Mr. Stauffer is going to be pressing any charges against you; he'll have plenty of his own problems to worry about. And I'm quite sure the authorities won't pursue the issue either. So, officially I'm telling you, don't do it again without notifying the police. But unofficially I can say that without you, Jimmy would still be locked in that room."

The woman smiled again at Laurie, and after a moment Laurie gave her a tremulous smile in return. Ms. Kamisar said, "I think we've covered everything. Let me call the hospital and find out if you can go and see Jimmy."

While she was on the phone, Laurie and Mark exchanged a look of relief; it sounded as if they weren't going to get into any legal trouble from what had happened last night. And it was good to hear that there was a plan to take care of little Jimmy.

Rachel Kamisar set down the receiver. "You can go and see Jimmy at the hospital now if you want. The nurses think it would be good for him."

"Oh, thanks," Laurie said. She stood up and then went on hesitantly, "You know, Ms. Kamisar, I feel like there's some kind of connection now between Jimmy and me. I'd like to—well, after he goes to a foster home do you think I could visit him sometimes, or maybe take him to the zoo or something?"

The gray-haired woman gazed searchingly at Laurie for a moment. Then she nodded. "I don't see why not. In fact, I think it might be important for both you and Jimmy." Coming around her desk, she walked with them to the door. "Give me a call in a couple of weeks and I'll let you know where Jimmy is."

She shook hands with Mark and then took Laurie's hand and held it for a moment. "Keep in touch, Laurie. I'd like to know how things go for you."

CHAPTER 17

"WELL, HOW WAS THE LITTLE BOY? DID they let you see him?" Laurie's father addressed his questions to both Laurie and Mark as they came into the house.

"Yes, they let me see him," Laurie answered slowly. "And I guess he's okay, at least physically. But he's still pretty scared and he doesn't exactly know what's going to happen to him next. I just hope they find him a nice foster family who'll help him try to forget the whole thing."

"Poor little guy." Mr. Carr shook his head. "That man—the boy's uncle—ought to be locked up for life. Seems to me that would be the proper punishment for doing that to a defenseless kid."

Laurie shuddered. "I can't stand to think about it—Jimmy must have felt so frightened and alone in that horrible little room. The nurse told me that they don't even know how long he was down there."

"Yeah, and he'd still be down there if it hadn't been for you," Mark said quietly.

Laurie's father frowned. "Well, I don't know about that. Of course, you did find him, but I guess it was just a coincidence, right?"

Laurie knew her dad didn't want to think about anything that seemed weird. He preferred to see the world as a logical, common-sense place where everything worked according to the rules. She would have been happy to let him believe his own version of last night's events. After all, it didn't really matter now. But Mark jumped in eagerly. "It wasn't just coincidence, Mr. Carr," he said in a positive tone. "Laurie had been hearing Jimmy call for help for a couple of weeks at least. Right, Laurie?"

Laurie nodded, remembering those pitiful cries that had awakened her so many times. No matter what her dad thought, she felt much better now that she knew those cries for help had been real, not some kind of bizarre product of her own imagination.

Mr. Carr was shaking his head. "I don't see how that could be," he told Mark doubtfully.

"Well, the way I figure it is that Laurie is especially sensitive to people who are unhappy or in trouble somehow," Mark explained with his usual enthusiasm. "It's like some kind of ESP. For some reason she has this fantastic ability to pick up on the strong emotions they are sending out. Of course, the connection is strongest when it's a person she knows and cares about, and I think the other voices she's heard in the past have all been people she was close to."

Laurie saw the dismayed look her father gave her. She knew he must be wondering what "other voices" Mark was talking about. In a way she wished Mark would stop explaining; she didn't want her dad to think she was totally off the wall. But at the same time she had to admit it was nice to hear someone speak so admiringly about her.

Mark was still talking to Mr. Carr. "I think Jimmy must have been so desperate that even though Laurie didn't know who he was or even that he existed, she could hear his calls for help."

"But if he was calling for help," Laurie's father asked, "why didn't the neighbors call the police?"

"Oh, I didn't mean he was actually calling out loud, though of course he might have been," Mark replied. "But I believe Laurie 'hears' the person's emotional message as if it were being said out loud."

Mr. Carr looked at Laurie. "Do you think that's true, Laurie? Did you really hear this little boy crying for help?"

"Yes, I did." Laurie chose her words with care. "I heard a child calling, 'Please help me, somebody help me.' I didn't know who it was, but one time when I heard it, I was sort of pulled toward that house. And last night I just knew that was where it was coming from."

"Well, I guess I have to admit that you turned out to be right," her father said unhappily. "But I don't understand how anyone can hear stuff that isn't being said. And why should you be the one to get some kind of weird messages or whatever you call them when people are in trouble? All I can say is I hope it won't ever happen again."

"I've got some books about ESP and stuff that I could lend you," Mark told Mr. Carr. "It's really interesting once you get into it. One expert says that people who can hear ESP-type messages are often feeling upset or unhappy themselves, and that makes them super sensitive or something. And lots of people who write about it say that the ability to receive these messages tends to fade as the person gets older." Mark smiled at Laurie. "So maybe you'll outgrow it and you'll just hear the usual boring stuff like us ordinary people."

"I guess I'll have to wait and see," Laurie said thoughtfully. "Because I don't have any control over it anyway."

Mr. Carr turned to Laurie and hugged her hard. "Well, honey, whatever reason you had for going to that house, I'm sure glad you're safe. It must have been pretty scary."

Laurie hugged him back. "It was more than scary, Dad, it was terrifying. But I'm okay now."

"That's my girl." Her dad smiled at her.

Looking up at her dad, Laurie realized how lucky she was. Even though Dad would always want to believe that her "voices" had some rational explanation if only he could think of it, Laurie knew he loved her without reservation.

"Listen, honey," he was saying, "you'd better call your mom. She's pretty worried about you."

When the phone rang at the other end, Laurie's mom picked it up right away. "Oh, Laurie, I'm so glad you called. How are you? Is everything okay? I was so upset when your dad called and told me what happened."

"Yeah, Mom, I'm fine."

Before she could go on, her mother broke in, "And what about the little boy? I haven't been able to stop thinking about him."

Soon Laurie was involved in explaining the whole story to her mother and answering Mom's horrified questions. When she got to the part about the meeting with Ms. Kamisar earlier that day, Mrs. Carr said, "Well, thank goodness he's got someone to look after him now."

"Yes, and I'm going to try to go visit him when he's been placed in a foster home," Laurie told her.

"Oh, good for you, honey." Mom drew a long breath. "This whole thing has been so frightening for you, hasn't it? I don't mean just last night, which goodness knows must have been scary enough, but all that time before when you didn't understand what was going on. You must have felt very much alone. But Laurie, I'm so proud of you—you didn't fall apart and you followed through on your instincts and did what you felt had to be done."

Laurie had a lump in her throat and for a moment she couldn't speak. At last she said huskily, "Thanks, Mom."

At the other end of the line she could hear her mother clear her throat. "Listen, honey, before all this happened there was something I wanted to ask you." She paused and then continued uncertainly, "You know my friend Andrea whose house in the mountains I borrowed a couple of weeks ago? Well, she's going to the Caribbean over Christmas vacation, and she's offered me her house. So I thought maybe you'd like to go up there with me for a week or so—it's supposed to be a great area for cross-country skiing, and we could . . . ?"

Her mother's voice trailed off into a question mark. Laurie's mind was spinning. What would it be like to spend a whole week alone with her mom? But before she had even thought it through, she heard herself saying enthusiastically, "Oh, Mom, that would be great!"

When she hung up, Laurie stood for a moment, thinking, What have I gotten myself into? But then she realized she hadn't felt the least bit awkward talking to Mom just now.

Christmas vacation would work out fine. In fact, Laurie was looking forward to it.

A short while later she was staring out the window of Mark's car as he drove toward the lake. Now that she and Mark were alone again, her thoughts returned to the whole sequence of strange events that had ended in the basement of that creepy old house. She wondered whether Mark was right. Would she "outgrow" her ability to receive ESP messages from unhappy people? In a way she hoped she would; life would be a lot more restful without any voices. But in another way she would regret losing that special sensitivity. After all, it had led her to Jimmy and had allowed her to help a child in trouble. She'd just have to wait and see what happened.

Mark parked under a big oak tree whose leaves had mostly fallen to lie in untidy heaps around the edges of the dirt parking lot. Without having to discuss it, the two of them began to walk along the path toward the big rock on the shoreline—"their" rock.

Mark scrambled up onto the flat surface and took Laurie's hands to pull her up next to him. They sat without speaking, looking out over the quiet gray water. Laurie felt Mark's arm go around her shoulders and pull her close. She felt a warm glow of contentment and thought, If Mark's expert is right and you have to be unhappy to hear voices, I sure won't be hearing any now.

She looked at Mark and found he was gazing at her, his brown eyes tender and almost solemn. Then he bent his head toward hers and their lips met in a kiss full of promise.